'Reading this book feels like stepping through a hushed and ornate museum, or a model village whose simulacrum of real life is so perfect as to be unsettling' *Observer*

'A family saga with below-stairs scenes, written in calm, decorous prose. It is also funny and moving, fully of surprises and challenging ideas ... Its evocation of the past offers many gifts of observation and psychological insight' *Times Literary Supplement*

'Compelling ... The novel's considered portrait of upper-class lives brings a Jamesian quality to this debut' *Irish Times*

'Beguiling ... A read to warm a winter evening' *Daily Mail*, Books of the Year

'Exquisite' *Metro*

'It's bloody brilliant' Guy

'An elegant, enthralling
this intimiste epic of soci... the years leading up to the
First World War. It has the lustre of life, beautiful and poignant'
Adam Foulds

'Super-assured ... Wholly convincing lives, described and written with great limpid precision of language' William Boyd

'A wonderful evocation of period – through language, clothes, objects – any reader will be irresistibly transported to Manchester and the lives of this strange Edwardian family' Tim Pears

'Immaculately written ... the detail and the dialogue are acutely rendered' *Literary Review*

'Strong on atmosphere ... Lyrical' *Tablet*

BY THE SAME AUTHOR

Short stories
The Burning Ground

Poetry
A Herring Famine
In the Flesh

ADAM O'RIORDAN is the author of two collections of poems, *In the Flesh* and *A Herring Famine*, and the short story collection *The Burning Ground*. He grew up in Manchester and later read English at Oxford, winning scholarships to do a Masters and PhD with Professor Andrew Motion at the University of London. After working in publishing for several years, he was appointed Poet-in-Residence at the Wordsworth Trust, the Centre for British Romanticism. His work has been awarded an Eric Gregory Award and a Somerset Maugham Award, shortlisted for the Ledbury Prize and longlisted for the Edge Hill Prize. Until 2019 he was Academic Director of Manchester Writing School and Programme Leader for the Creative Writing MA/MFA.

adamoriordan.com

THE FALLING THREAD

ADAM O'RIORDAN

BLOOMSBURY PUBLISHING
LONDON · OXFORD · NEW YORK · NEW DELHI · SYDNEY

BLOOMSBURY PUBLISHING
Bloomsbury Publishing Plc
50 Bedford Square, London, WC1B 3DP, UK
29 Earlsfort Terrace, Dublin 2, Ireland

BLOOMSBURY, BLOOMSBURY PUBLISHING and the Bloomsbury Publishing logo are
trademarks of Bloomsbury Publishing Plc

First published in Great Britain 2021
This edition published 2022

ISBN: HB: 978-1-4088-5653-6; PB: 978-1-4088-5655-0;
EBOOK: 978-1-4088-5654-3; EPDF: 978-1-5266-4511-1

2 4 6 8 10 9 7 5 3 1

Typeset by Integra Software Services Pvt. Ltd.
Printed and bound in Great Britain by CPI Group (UK) Ltd, Croydon CR0 4YY

MIX
Paper | Supporting
responsible forestry
FSC® C171272

To find out more about our authors and books visit www.bloomsbury.com
and sign up for our newsletters

For the rain it raineth every day.
Shakespeare, *Twelfth Night*, Act 5, scene i

To J&A

The star shell burst, making clear the jagged shapes;
scorched tree trunks, the ruined buildings along the
Armentières—Wez Macquart road. There was a moment of
quiet then the barrage started again, a Lewis gun stuttering
further up the line.

'For you, sir.' The sergeant tossed the letter to him. 'Should
have been here last week but some hold-up with BAPO.'

'Thanks, Maguire. This doesn't seem to be lifting – you
should find cover.'

He pulled off his mitten with his teeth. He was shaking
slightly. There was a rat crouched beside the sandbags on the
flooded slats outside. It looked at him, blinking.

Dear Lieut. Wright,
Husband on leave from War Office so have come to
Windermere. Your father showed us some photographs
from camp and explained your squadron had been
dismounted but others were stuck over in Ireland or
making do with bicycles. We've sent a parcel we hope
might be of use; shaving brush, razor, chocolate and

some good (inexpensive) cigarettes. Aunt Eloise
telegrammed to inform us …

*The blast sent a tin mug flying from the table as soil spilled
from the boards of the dugout. He could feel the barrage moving
closer. He stuffed the letter into his pocket.*

*Last time Maguire had taken him by the shoulders and told
him to count. If he got to a thousand he'd have made it.*

He shut his eyes beginning one, two, three …

1890

August

He should have seen her by now. He had already idled over breakfast, the tails of his kippers hardening on his plate. He looked down at the newspaper, its report of Rhodes's attack on Matabeleland. He imagined the piles of flyblown bodies festering in the sun, then glanced at how England might fare in the second test: big, druidic Grace still smarting from that golden duck. Yes, where was she?

At the top of the house her bedroom door was open. On the dressing table a box covered in seashells, an upturned hairbrush. There was a faint indentation running the length of the bed. He closed his eyes and breathed the scent he recognised as hers. Nothing heavy or complex like the fragrances his mother wore with their base notes of opoponax and vanilla. This was similar to the smell that clings to cut lavender, a sour edge endowing it with something human. He leaned in just enough to decide the room was empty. Perhaps he would find her downstairs in the drawing room, at the piano. Of course, the piano.

It was here, a month ago, he began to notice his sisters' new governess, Miss Greenhalgh, bending to their questions;

hands over theirs as she asked them to repeat a phrase. He might have recorded her species and genus, like the naturalist he believed himself to be. What would he have noted? Freckles – colour of honey or weak tea. Eyes – green with flecks of amber, disorderly, around the pupil. Lashes – thick across the upper lid, sparse on the lower. The smallish bosom. Age – twenty, twenty-two at most.

Charles stood in a patch of sunlight by the piano, *Jungennamen's Exercises* open on the rosewood stand. He tried to decipher a bar, humming as he scanned the room; Father's ammonites lined along the mantelpiece, Mother's music box with its blurry rendition of 'The Blue Danube'. Miss Greenhalgh was not here. He would try the kitchen.

Cook removed a lump of dough from the mixing bowl as she pushed the cat away with her shin. It staggered on the stone floor, letting out a dry, constricted miaow.

She nodded at Charles as she began to work, pale wrists ploughing the yellowish dough. Besides her and the cat, the kitchen was empty.

'Wish to go outside, do you, pussykin?' Charles said. He opened the kitchen door and the cat poured itself through the gap.

The garden was very bright after the kitchen. Charles stood waiting for the world to take shape: the high row of poplars, the wide lawn drained of colour for a moment then intensely present. He saw Miss Greenhalgh sitting at a folding wooden butler's table. He inspected himself in the window. Acceptable, he thought. Perhaps the check of his trousers was a little loud, clearly bought at Pauldens and not in the capital. Still, his waistcoat was from London. Yes, he was acceptable.

As he reached her table he felt the words come too quickly.

'Miss Greenhalgh, shall we, I mean, well, would you care to take a stroll?'

She looked up, shielding her eyes from the sun.

They walked along the gravel path beside the lawn, past the ageratum with its powder-blue flowers, the neatly tended nasturtiums. A bird was whipping a snail shell against the edge of the path, pecking at the glittering insides.

'*Turdus philomelos*,' Charles said, 'the song thrush.'

'We called them throstles.' She paused, then said, 'I suppose you know the name for everything, don't you?'

Charles felt a burning in his cheeks, his scrotum tightening faintly.

'Mama gave me a book when I was young, offered me a small sum if I could learn a few. Animalia, Chordata, Aves. We have Linnaeus to thank ... ' He saw he was losing her. 'But throstles is much better. Tell me, Miss Greenhalgh, have the girls shown you the wild garden?'

She shook her head, then said, 'Hettie, please.'

At the far end of the lawn they paused beside an old glasshouse. The paint on the ironwork had begun to flake; grass flourished in the guttering.

'Familiar?'

She shook her head again.

'Built to mirror the house. Well, that's the story,' he said, peering in at a bending column of flowerpots.

'Wild garden's this way.'

Charles slid himself behind the back of the glasshouse.

'Come through,' he called out from the other side.

The glasshouse gave on to a clearing: scrubby grass, a black circle from a bonfire, with a dense thicket running in a curve around it. There was a scythe and an old hand mower. Charles picked up a bamboo cane and began hacking at the weeds, tiny seed heads exploding. He felt the silence coagulate. Miss Greenhalgh stood a few yards away as if expecting to receive some formal instruction from him.

'Well, you can say you've seen it now,' he said eventually, setting down the bamboo cane and wiping his hands.

They were back at the butler's table in the middle of the lawn.

'So why are you not with your family?'

'I'm supposed to be travelling. To Engadine and the baths at St Moritz. But alas, I have been delayed.' Charles exhaled theatrically. He talked about his growing frustration at the delay, and his travelling companion and school friend, Angus Bird.

'And how long will you be with us for?' he asked.

'Well, that depends somewhat.'

'Until they have mastered a sonata or two?'

'Oh yes, at least that long I should think. Your mother sent word I'm to travel to join them in Windermere tomorrow.'

'She has tired of the girls already,' Charles said.

Hettie smiled very softly.

'Your sisters tell me you are studying at Cambridge.'

He felt his carousel of anecdote engage: the oily vice master, the underfunded laboratories, the young lady over at Newnham who had obtained the top score in the Mathematical Tripos and the little swell of outrage and indignation this had caused.

As Charles talked, his hand moved towards Hettie, thrown out to convey amusement at the story he was telling, until the tips of two fingers rested on the flesh below her thumb. A bee lurched from behind a spear of blue larkspur at the edge of the lawn. The pair watched as it zigzagged towards them, circling the table. Hettie narrowed her eyes, tried to shoo it, awkwardly, unnaturally, using only her free hand, the hand Charles was not touching.

*

In this light the scar looked even more livid, purple at its edges and puckered like the anus of a cat. Charles rebuked himself for the comparison. But he was certain that it was connected to, indeed the cause of, the new maid's slurred speech. He had read a treatise on oral deformities and tried to recall the detail.

'Thank you,' Charles said, rising from the chair to take the letter. Susannah, he thought, he must remember to use her name. 'Thank you, Susannah,' he said with an emphasis that made her pause. Then she nodded, the glossy knot of her lip twitching. At Cambridge he had observed an electrical current pass through the leg of a frog on a dissection table; it came back to him now.

Charles tore open the envelope. As he unfolded the note certain words swam up at him. There had been silence for days from Bird; they had already missed their planned date of departure. Charles learned Bird was returning early to Cambridge, an unforeseen condition of the exhibition he had been awarded. There would be no trip to the baths at St Moritz. No walking in Engadine among the alpine flowers and undulating grassland they had sat in his rooms talking of earnestly all last term. The letter assured Charles their trip was not cancelled, merely postponed. Bird had written to the owner of the guest house, who had promised them lodgings, if they wished, at Easter. Bird would cover any expenses incurred in preparing for the trip. Charles knew this could not be true. How could it be when he had subsidised Angus all last term at the Kestrel Club after they were elected members?

'We'll be off now.'

Charles looked up. Cook and Susannah were standing a few feet away.

'The band,' Cook said.

He stared at them blankly.

'The Thornhill Temperance.'

'Yes,' he said without any conviction.

'Your mother said before she left … '

'Of course.'

Cook was wearing her own clothes, a heavy plaid skirt, a white blouse, a faded blue silk bonnet. Charles had never seen her without her apron. She looked younger. Susannah stood beside her, dressed much the same as before save a tatty length of ribbon in her hair like something snagged in a hedgerow.

'Well,' Charles said, trying to think of words to fill the widening silence, 'I hope they acquit themselves creditably.'

So this was to be his summer. The society of Cook and Susannah; the *Proceedings of the Academy of Natural Sciences* for stimulation. Or a train to Windermere, conversations with his father about the new steam launch, pendulum rods, pitman arms; suppers with the neighbours; Knowles the gardener rackety and bent double calling to take the young master out to engage in some ritualised mammalian killing; his sisters, the unceasing Tabitha and Eloise, who had recently elected him Authority on Everything, their own encyclopedia to be consulted at all times, no matter too small. Remaining here in Manchester would mean the Hare or the Turk's Head with Caraway – pompous after two years of employment – perhaps a fitful correspondence with Bird. He looked up from the armchair to see Hettie collecting her music from the stand by the piano. He felt desire sluice through him, imagining her soft body under that soufflé of petticoats. He lifted Bird's letter to the light.

'You have a letter.'

He pretended not to have heard her.

'I'm sorry?'

'A letter. You have one, I see.'

'Ah, yes,' he said gravely.

'From your friend Bird?'

'Alas.'

'And the news is not good?'

'No.' Charles paused. 'But a letter from Bird,' he said, displaying his indefatigable spirit, 'is never without consolations, no matter how dire the news.'

Charles had risen from the armchair and was leaning on the mantelpiece where he lit a cigarette. He felt the rich smoke settle him. He blew onto the match, tossing it into the hearth.

'In my room there are other letters you are sure to find amusing. When Bird sets his mind to it,' he said, taking one of his father's ammonites and holding it to the light, 'he can move his reader from tears to laughter as quickly as any stage comic.'

He studied her expression through the delicate skein of blue smoke.

'You may see also how his signature has changed over the course of our correspondence, it now takes up a quarter of any letter's final page, a remarkable extravagance when his frugality in all other matters is considered.'

He had built the trap and now he baited it.

'Perhaps I might show you some later?'

*

The lugworms had been found dead on the beach a few yards from the colony, ten miles to the north-east of Cape May on the New Jersey Coast, *having perchance left their burrow in the endeavour to reach the water*. The essay built on work Charles had seen by Stimpson. These were the cigar-shaped polychaete he had been charged with bettering his understanding of by his tutor Piggot-Roche. Slurry brown with a delicate green sheen, the colour of something a newborn baby might expel.

The afternoon had so far been spent working in his father's study on his essay on '*Arenicola cristata* and their Allies: salinity, embryology, span of life'. When he began to tire Charles had sketched a lugworm in the margin of his notebook, and beside it the cigar the creature was said to resemble. He had looked down at the scribblings, placed a cross beside the lugworm and tick beside the cigar. 'Piggot-Roche be damned,' he said as if it were a formal leave-taking required of him.

It was four when Hettie came to his room. The clocks around the house were striking their final chimes. She hesitated at the door. Charles was lying on his bed, sending rings of smoke towards the ceiling, the *Proceedings of the*

Academy open on the floor. Hettie looked around the room; the walls were crowded with watercolours, above the fireplace a vase of white roses, their petals beginning to brown.

'So these letters then.'

'The letters, yes, of course.'

'You have a great number of pictures.'

Charles turned from the trunk at the foot of the bed.

'By a friend. This one,' he said, pointing, 'is based on a work by Sargent. *Fumée d'Ambre Gris.*'

He wished for a moment the other members of the Kestrel Club could see him. He set down his cigar, glad be rid of it, and wiped his hands on his trousers.

'And beside it, there, is an etching of the Ponte Vecchio. Bird and I visited last summer.' He removed the etching from the picture rail and sat with it on his lap.

He made no mention of the anxiety of the trip, Angus's sickness, the panic they felt as strangers in the foreign city. He gestured for Hettie to come and sit with him. She paused, for what seemed a long time, then approached, the door swinging shut behind her. He was aware of the heat of her body as their shoulders touched, the etching balanced on his lap, their faces reflected in the glass. Moments later they heard Cook and Susannah return, laughter from downstairs, Cook imitating a trumpet.

He set his finger on the first window of the building that ran along the bridge.

'Allow me to introduce you,' he said, tapping the glass. 'Here lives Signor ... Contandio –' his tongue tripped over the consonants – 'a sad and solemn fellow if ever I met one, and here the widowed sisters Donata and Trisola, great beauties in their day, would you believe?'

The sun made prominent the down on her cheek. He leaned over and kissed her. It was unlike the others. The girl in Florence who tasted of tobacco, who took him back to the room above a *macelleria*, a few thin and iridescent cuts of meat in the window. The woman he had visited with Caraway last winter, hitching up her skirt until it revealed the lower half of her wide white body, the crimped circlet of marks across her belly, who laughed as he withdrew, standing in his shirt tails, his look of shock.

He kissed her again, felt her tongue dart back in response. He began to undress her, hurriedly, greedily, his fingers at the curve of her shoulders, her bare arms. She pulled him in towards her as the room shrank and enclosed them. The leisurely contralto of a blackbird on its perch in the garden growing louder and louder until it seemed to fill the entire room.

September

September

The crane fly drifted upwards, weightlessly trailing its wire-fine legs. When it gained the maximum height possible, near the pelmet, it proceeded to cast itself against the glass, determined to pass off into the sky evident yet unreachable beyond. It seemed a strange remnant of the summer: the insect hatching late, now rushing to devour whatever was left for it of the world. Charles watched its efforts from the button-back bergère in his father's study, a shawl wrapped around his shoulders. He had made the room his own, colonising the space in the weeks after Hettie left for Windermere. An apple core lay browning beside a saucer of raisins.

He was behind this morning, and every time he felt he had arrived at something close to clarity the thought seemed to escape him. He blamed Caraway squarely for his predicament: the headache, the waves of nausea, the abject lack of progress with his reading. He imagined the look of reproach on Piggot-Roche's face, the tut-tutting from that prim little mouth.

Yesterday Caraway had greeted him outside his father's offices; a shining terracotta building opposite the Ottoman Bank. Charles was late, having stopped to buy a newspaper. A man had shot himself during the morning service at St Paul's. Caraway was leaning against the massive doors, studded with knuckles of iron. He had run to fat since school; a recently cultivated moustache lent him an air of calculated melancholy.

He seized Charles's elbow and ushered him inside, up the narrow staircase, its iron banister worn smooth. Charles let his hand skim along it as they ascended.

'We shan't be long,' Caraway promised, before talking with gravity about the new duties his father had recently given to him. They entered a high-ceilinged room with what looked like an altar table at one end where a dozen men were gathered. Charles assumed these must be the commercial travellers over whom Caraway now had responsibility. Above the table was a leaded glass dome that cast a harsh light on the men's faces, some raw and blotched, others yellow and wan.

'Here to collect their samples,' Caraway explained.

A parcel, the size of a hay bale, had been sliced open: a ragged gash down its front and from inside batches of napkins and cloths had been laid along the table.

'My office is over there,' Caraway said, 'in the south transept, and Father's is up there in the High Place. All alone in his apse and sacristy.'

As Caraway approached the men their chatter diminished.

'Gentlemen,' Caraway said after giving a short speech on the quality of the new goods, 'I shall leave you to Mrs Ketley who will introduce the latest lines.'

A woman in black, a mass of dry hair pinned above her head, stood, knotting and unknotting her hands as if they were pieces of a puzzle that would not mesh. Charles watched Caraway's smile dissolve as he walked back towards him.

'Apes to a man,' Caraway whispered. In the stairway he paused, leaning his large frame against the cool of the green-and-white mosaic tiles. 'Now, apes, trained apes, selling Father's goods. There's an idea I must raise with him.'

The pair retreated to the Turk's Head, a short walk from the office. The bar was crowded. At the far end was a macaw in a brass cage. It moved crabwise along its perch, rocking and dipping its head. Caraway pushed his way to the front of the bar, pulling Charles behind him.

'Two pints of Empress,' Caraway said. As the girl set down the glasses of porter, the colour of wet earth, he lit a cheroot, scrutinising the tip. He took a playbill from his pocket and smoothed it out across the bar. He ran a finger down the list of troupes performing that month.

'They'll be the end of me, Charlie,' he said, glancing from the playbill, 'but I just adore those *jolies-petites* and their fancy dancing.'

Charles laughed half-heartedly.

'Laugh, Charlie,' he continued, 'but I have it on good authority these girls are told to seek out Hewlett Caraway on arrival in Manchester.'

The brass pumps caught his reflection, offering it back warped and in triplicate. When the girl looked over Caraway gave a wide grin.

'Plate of mutton chops and a dozen oysters,' he said emphatically.

The Empress evened the mood of the two friends but by his fourth glass Caraway had grown maudlin.

'So easily spoiled, Charlie, gifts each time I visit their lodgings. Best part of a pound just for a touch. Expensive business what with all the bonbons and trinketry. What Father would call a loss-making enterprise.'

The head on Caraway's Empress made Charles think of the scum that builds against an inlet or a harbour wall. He watched as Caraway sucked it away, wiping his lips then giving the tip of his nose a pinch.

'Tell me, are you love-sick, Charlie, or simply lust-struck?'

'What are you talking about?'

'Well, while I've been busily trying to seduce *cum oculis meis* –' he nodded to the barmaid – 'you're yet to return a single glance from her.'

He hooked his arm around Charles's neck and pulled him close.

'Yes, I can smell it on you.'

Charles pushed Caraway off and straightened his collar.

'Some malmsey-nosed hedge-creeper.'

'Don't be ridiculous.'

'Who is it this time, the gardener's daughter? One of Mother's maids?' Caraway paused, reassessing the situation. 'No, I have this wrong, don't I?'

He screwed up the playbill and tossed it at the barmaid's feet.

'She's squatting in your head, this dollymop, and try as you may you cannot make her leave.'

Charles hesitated and as soon as he did he knew it to be fatal. He looked at the caged macaw, the mechanical movement of its scarred and slate-blue beak.

'For God's sake, Caraway.'

Caraway's expression was beginning to slacken. He went to signal for more porter but Charles caught his arm.

Yes, Hewlett Caraway was squarely to blame for Charles's state this morning. He hoped he wasn't coming down with something. He had worked too hard this summer not to return triumphant, better read than any of his peers, the apple of Piggot-Roche's eye. He would steel himself – not sick, just the worse for all that porter. He pulled himself up in the bergère, breathing slowly. He heard the hansom come to a halt outside. The high sharp yapping of his mother's dogs as they spilled from the cab, gravel flying from under their paws as they raced towards the front door. He could hear his sisters Eloise and Tabitha, their voices raised in shrill dispute:

'That is not the case,' Tabitha was saying. 'That is simply not the case.'

Could they really be back already? Had the weeks passed so quickly? He looked at the books from his college library, felt a pitiful sense of having failed to extract all that he needed.

On the driveway his sisters ran to him, arms flung open, colliding with such force that Charles stumbled backwards. Hettie was gathering her things from inside the hansom she had travelled in with his sisters. She wore a grey three-cornered shawl that emphasised her paleness. She was carrying her music case. She walked past him and into the house.

'Charles, have you been smoking?' Tabitha asked, clinging to him, straining her neck as she leaned back from where she had taken a lungful of his coat.

'Do you admire her shawl?' Eloise asked, pointing towards Hettie. 'We've been working on our own.'

'Yes,' Tabitha said, 'with Berlin wool Mama sent for from Kendal.'

At his mother's instruction Cook laid on a large lunch: fish soup, from a French recipe, served in a big tureen and flavoured with cayenne and anchovy sauce; a plate of cold chicken, boiled eggs in a silver bowl, a salad of crinkly-leafed watercress, two freshly baked loaves.

Eloise and Tabitha were taking turns telling stories from Windermere; about the steam launch; about the daughters of neighbours, and about the good match one of these daughters might some day make for Charles.

'There is one young lady, Charles,' Tabitha said. 'Her engagement to the son of a farmer –'

'No, that's not true, he was –'

'Do hush, Eloise – has been called off. She is twenty-six,' Tabitha said, peeling the shell from a boiled egg, the shattered fragments clinging to the membrane; the air hung with sulphur.

'An old bat with her nose always in a book we thought just perfect for you,' said Eloise, stymieing her sister's story as she reached across for another piece of cake.

Charles's mother set down a vase of flowers, cupping the heads until she was satisfied with how they fell. Dolly, the housemaid, came to the table to tell them Hettie was being sick.

'Oh,' Charles's mother said as if she had just received terrible news. Then turned to Dolly more softly. 'Send Susannah for Dr Calthorpe.'

'Mama, must you call for Calthorpe? Give the poor man some peace. Remember when you had him over last for Father. I'm sure the poor girl's malady will pass – calling the doctor seems extravagant given the circumstances.'

*

27

The undertaking had the air of a parlour game in which both participants had lost interest but continued to gratify their hosts. Dr Calthorpe had placed three chairs in the bay window, instructing Hettie to lie across the makeshift assemblage. Charles stood at the foot of the stairs, looking in through the part-open door, panic rising as the doctor placed his hand across Hettie's abdomen, applying pressure in various positions as he looked out of the window. After the initial examination, Dr Calthorpe asked Dolly to bring him a bowl of boiled water. Eventually he emerged, wiping his hands on a handkerchief, and suggested Charles and his parents join him in the dining room. Dr Calthorpe positioned himself at the head of the table. As he spoke he moved his hands as if dealing cards, as if the small party were seated for a game of canasta.

'As I suspected,' Dr Calthorpe said, 'the girl is with child, although at a fairly early stage. Now, you will excuse my impertinence but I've spoken with her and she contends, having been with no others,' he continued in his cloying, slipper-soft Edinburgh accent, 'that young Charles here is the father.' He glanced across the table at him. 'Now, as I say, she is at a very early stage, so much might still go wrong.'

Charles felt a prickling along his shins, his palms beginning to tingle. He imagined standing and bolting through the door. He felt he had it within his power to run for miles, until the river met the estuary, where his father had taken him when the plans for the Ship Canal were taking shape.

He could swim until England was reduced to a line on the horizon. In the sea, sink to the bottom, his flesh picked apart by soft-mouthed creatures, as the tides moved above him.

'Much might still go wrong,' Dr Calthorpe repeated, lowering his head this time, tracing the outline of his face in the polished table with his thumb.

His mother had grown pale. His father stood, offering his hand to Dr Calthorpe. When the three of them were alone, Charles's father removed his pocket watch and set it on the table. His mother was working her thumbs inside a handkerchief. She toyed with it, then she pressed it with great force into her mouth.

*

'Has she been sick again?' Tabitha asked.

'Is she going to die?' Eloise added gleefully.

Charles's sisters looked up at him with open, expectant faces. They were standing by the piano in matching day dresses. A stye was beginning to form on Eloise's right eye, the pouch of skin tight and shining, lending her a drowsy, partially dazed look. Charles hushed the girls, batting the air with his hands. He steered them out of the drawing room into the hallway where he hoped Dolly or Susannah might find them and return them to their rooms. After Dr Calthorpe left, Charles's mother and father had retreated: his mother to her bedroom, his father to his study. Charles had stood outside the study door listening to his father repeatedly clearing his throat.

'Away with you,' Charles said weakly to his sisters who were lingering in the hallway. He took a seat by the fire. His legs felt stiff, like a pair of wooden spoons. There was a book on the arm of the chair, his mother's *Waverley*. He opened it on his lap, grateful to have a place to direct his attention. It had fallen open at the banquet scene. '*The Baron ate like a famished soldier.*' Charles heard the words but they made no sense. He tried again, '*The Baron ate like a famished soldier,*' then a gap appeared, a numbness, no meaning.

He saw Tabitha whispering to her sister, her hand pressed against Eloise's cheek. A few seconds later Eloise was standing before him with the beginnings of a smile.

'Now,' she said, 'it is only fair, Charles, that you tell us.' She glanced to her sister, as she fought to contain her laughter. 'Tabitha wants to know: is it you that has killed our new governess?'

Eloise slapped her hand against her mouth, steadying herself on the armchair. Charles was suddenly on his feet. He slammed the book onto the floor, and struck the table with his flailing arm. A bowl of potpourri shattered as it hit the floor. The pages in the *Waverley* had come away from their binding. Eloise ran to Tabitha. Charles saw a look of bewilderment on their faces. He left the book where it had fallen by the shattered bowl, petals and barks releasing their fragrances. His sisters recoiled as he passed. Eloise sobbed. Tabitha held her, an arm around her back, glowering at Charles with all the spite she could muster.

On reaching his bedroom he closed the door and locked it. He stood, eyes shut, fists at his side. He rocked back against the door, slammed his skull hard against it. It was after dark when Charles left his room. He walked to the kitchen and watched Cook plucking a hen. She brought a cleaver down across its neck, tossed its head into the mass of feathers in the basket below.

'You're welcome to take over,' she said.

The next day Charles was called to his father's study. On the desk was a book on anatomy, torn from its wrapper. A line drawing of a foetus; soft limbs curled in on itself and, despite the elongated dome of the head, clearly visible as a human form. He did not invite Charles to sit.

'We have never preached monasticism, nor even the strict avoidance of life's spontaneous pleasures.' His voice trailed off then and he seemed to lose his appetite for a sermon. 'We have come to a decision.' He looked down at the line drawing. 'You accept that you are old enough to be accountable for your actions?'

Charles nodded.

'Then you will marry her. And go away for a year.'

Charles tried not to betray any sign that the news affected him.

'If we act with haste, the match might even be made public.'

There were tears running down his father's cheeks.

*

The doctor had tried to explain what was wrong. He was suggesting she be moved to a place where she could be better looked after. Hettie watched him as he spoke, his large head, the coating of dried skin on the shoulders of his jacket. Talking slowly as if to a child or an intelligent animal. It was his third visit in the space of a week. She nodded, then Mrs Wright said, 'He means the infirmary.' She felt another wave of nausea and bit down on her cheeks.

Dolly helped her pack. It hadn't taken very long.

'I'll take these down,' Dolly said as if disappointed at how little she possessed.

'Yes, thank you.'

She looked around the room, the small window, the narrow bed. She felt light-headed and had to sit. Dolly came back and helped her downstairs. A cab was waiting. She wondered if someone might accompany her. But then who?

She presented herself at the infirmary and waited for the doctor. He seemed altered here, less attentive. He led her along a ward to a place that was more like a stockroom or a large cupboard. 'Someone will be along presently,' he said. 'There's a receptacle should you need it.' He gestured to an enamel kidney dish on the floor. She put her case down and lay, fully clothed, on the bed.

She began to think about her father, the few times each
year he took the cart track into the city. She had gone with
him as a girl. From the moor she had seen the city for
the first time, like the aftermath of some catastrophe; the
massed chimneys, their low hanging smoke, the blues of
the wet slate roofs. It was years before she left their village
again. Setting off for school with her sisters each morning
on the long walk. In summer the bog cotton, white heads
trembling in the breeze. The schoolroom in the former
piggery and the square piano with the broken cabinet and
scuffed legs, donated by one of the reforming men.

She knew as they gathered around the piano, the school-
mistress, the reforming men, that she was not as good
as they willed her to be. Nonetheless at fifteen she had
gone to Manchester to lodge with a musician at the Halle
Orchestra, who had studied at the Vienna Conservatory.
Her father signed a deed of release. She would keep house
for a kitchen maid's wage and a few hours' tuition each
week. They stuck to it for the first month, the musician
impatient, distracted, once he gauged the limits of her abil-
ity. She feared she would be returned to the moor. Instead
the musician offered her a *Wahlurlaubstag*, an afternoon
every week 'to spend as you please', he said, looking up
from the breakfast table.

'If you are sure?'

'Yes, of course, go.'

*

It was the year of the Royal Jubilee Exhibition. Everything imaginable manufactured, from ornate porcelains to the state umbrella of a West African king. She would pay a shilling every Thursday. So much of everything at the exhibition, so little back at the musician's rooms. His life barely touched the place. He was away most of the week in London or touring. Very occasionally he would have guests, a Herr Vetter, a Herr Tenenbaum, a Mrs Smithem who once came with a piece by Dvořák. He introduced her to them as his pupil. He might have said cook or housekeeper. He might have said kitchen maid. 'A pupil,' Mrs Smithem said, lightly clapping her fingertips. 'You must have her play.' And so she had, on the clicking, discoloured keys of the ancient Zumpe piano. Polite applause, then emphatic, guttural German, back and forth between the guests. Later an invitation to play for Mrs Smithem at her home, and, once she had proved herself pleasant and unobtrusive company, to come and instruct the Smithem children in some rudiments of the pianoforte. 'You must be bored out of your wits,' Mrs Smithem said, 'alone in those rooms all week, it cannot be sanitary for a young lady.'

First *pupil*, now *lady*. She was seventeen and felt like a commodity. It pleased her to be traded from household to household. She came with a provenance, a history that was irrevocably hers, the former pupil of a graduate of the Vienna Conservatory. How indelible it felt. Moving through the fashionable neighbourhoods, accruing renown at each address. Treated like a distant cousin by the families. She possessed these homes more intimately than their inhabitants.

At the infirmary, they had given her a mug of watery cocoa and some wafer biscuits. Later a nurse had come and under the doctor's instruction applied a liniment of morphia. There would be a purgative each morning, the doctor told her, and she would be restricted to her bed. 'Think yourself lucky,' he said, 'I know of colleagues who until recently were applying leeches with a speculum.' He let his gaze fall on her legs beneath the sheet, and briefly touched his top lip with his tongue. 'The nurse here will be back in the morning to give your aperient.'

The first night she had sensed the doctor at the foot of her bed. She had lain still, pretending to sleep. She felt his face close to hers, could smell eau de vie and the cardamom musk of his sweat. For a moment she was certain he was about to lean in and kiss her. In the morning, after administering the purgative, the nurse made a tent of her sheets with an outstretched arm. She felt the edge of the bedpan against her buttocks. 'Up you get.' She braced her hands against the bed frame, shoulders hunched. She felt clumsy and vulgar. The nurse pulled the bedpan from under her, glancing at the contents as she carried it from the room.

*

The infirmary's stonework was coarsened with soot, there were narrow columns in its portico, porthole windows in the dome. Charles and his mother mounted the pavement behind a row of cabs. His mother was wearing a fox-fur stole, beads of moisture trapped between the russet hairs. The smell made Charles think of the badger sett he saw flushed as a boy. He had seen braces of pheasant hung above the range, had watched his mother as she wept at the burial of one her lapdogs, a black-eyed schipperke, which had taken itself to a corner of the garden to expire. But the badger was the first creature he watched die. He credited the event with attracting him to the study of the Natural Sciences. In truth, he only remembered his fear for the terriers as they shot down into the dark, and his disgust as the twitching, wheezing half-killed animal was hauled above ground.

The cabmen were gathered in a circle, the burr of their accents from the north of the city. 'It never, it never is,' one of them was saying. They were discussing a patch on the horse of the front-most cab. A cabman, hatless, hair thinning at his pale crown, broke from the group and worked his thumb into the horse's hindquarter as if the mange were a fleck of paint that could be rubbed away. In the distance beyond the cabmen Charles saw Dr Calthorpe.

'Mama,' Charles said, in the voice of his younger self, the voice he felt shamed into using. His mother called out 'Calthorpe', as if summoning one of her dogs. Her words lost in the clamour of the afternoon. She called again, her voice shrill, almost operatic. Charles felt a prickling heat across the tops of his ears. The cabmen stopped their conversation. Dr Calthorpe turned on his heels, raising a hand like an umpire signalling a bye. 'We shall have him report now, I think,' Charles's mother said.

They walked across the courtyard of the infirmary, past two porters standing by a handcart covered in a grubby tarpaulin, and a nurse showing another objects on her chatelaine. As they entered the infirmary Dr Calthorpe nodded to a colleague, then escorted Charles and his mother towards the Men's Amputation Ward.

'The most direct route, but also, I dare say, fairly educational.'

Dr Calthorpe brought them to a halt at the head of the ward. There were curtains open at the tall windows. A low moaning broken by fits of coughing. In the closest bed was a man in his twenties; standing he must have been over six feet tall. His cheeks were sunken, his hair prematurely white in patches. He scratched at the space where his right arm should be. Dr Calthorpe raised a finger in admonishment and the man slumped back against the iron bedhead.

'Osteomyelitis,' Dr Calthorpe said. 'A simple procedure. A pity that we could not save more of the limb.'

In the next bed along was an older man. He was unshaven, the waterlines of his eyes ringed pink. Dr Calthorpe turned to Charles.

'Both legs amputated above the knee,' he said as if pointing out a common plant in a hothouse. 'Fell into an unfenced mule. As you may have observed at your father's factories,' Dr Calthorpe said, 'the mills are kept humid to preserve the cotton. Our friend is near deaf from the machines and he also, it saddens me to say, suffers from fairly advanced byssinosis. And now this.' He gazed at the space where the man's legs should be, gesturing for Charles and his mother to move closer. The stumps were bound tightly in bandages, under a small linen tent. He lay staring across at the empty bed next to him. Charles watched the stumps twitch. At the end of the ward a nurse began drawing the curtains shut with a brass hook on a long wooden pole.

'They must sleep each afternoon,' Dr Calthorpe said, 'else they will never mend.'

As they left, Charles glanced back. He saw the tall man with the missing arm lighting a cigarette, then another man, and then another, until a dozen glowing orange points of light filled the artificial darkness.

The room was windowless, not quite the private quarters Dr Calthorpe had assured them would be most efficacious to Hettie's recovery, those constant fits of vomiting, *hyperemesis gravidarum*, he called it. There was a wardrobe, a mirror above the bed and a faded four-panel Oriental screen, with geishas by a pagoda. Hettie lay with a sheet pulled up over her.

'My own rooms,' Dr Calthorpe said, 'are very close by.'

He looked down at Hettie.

'We shall wake her now, I think.'

*

Dr Calthorpe withdrew, his head bowed. Charles's mother lingered inspecting herself in the mirror, adjusting her stole with the air of a woman who has dropped in at a department store to idle away an hour before an engagement.

'Mama, please.'

She called after Dr Calthorpe who was talking with the nurses outside. Charles dragged a wicker chair towards the bed. There was a thick crocheted blanket across the foot, a metal kidney dish on the floor.

'Dr Calthorpe is looking after you, I trust?'

Hettie closed her eyes and nodded, pushing herself up against the pillows.

'He says you must stay hydrated.'

Charles reached for the jug of water. He filled the glass to the brim then sipped away the excess. 'Here, drink some.'

She lifted her head to meet the rim of the glass. There was muffled laughter from the nurses outside.

'Dr Calthorpe was kind enough to give us a tour of one of the wards ... The girls ask after you. They continue to practise.'

Hettie suddenly covered her mouth. Charles picked up the kidney dish from the floor, but she shook her head.

'Perhaps you would like me to tell you of our plans?'

She did not respond.

Charles reached for the glass of water. He noticed a small mark where Hettie's mouth had touched it, imprinting the edge with the contours of her lower lip.

*

39

The porter Dr Calthorpe arranged to show them out moved with an awkward, sloping gait as if he had damaged some part of his pelvis. Charles wondered if the man had once been a patient at the infirmary, the venereal section or the fever ward or perhaps an unknown wing reserved for some special infirmity bred here in the city.

Along the corridor gas lamps hissed, the shadows of their fixtures thrown onto the sticky-looking flaxseed-coloured cellulose. A girl in a wicker-backed wheelchair was pushed past. Her hair was cut around a broad oval face, spittle drying at the corners of her mouth. The nurse pushing her smiled at the porter then at Charles's mother who ignored her. They had been in the infirmary too long. They needed air, fresh air; even the smoke-laced, mizzle-drenched Manchester air would feel cleansing.

Eventually the corridor gave onto a vestibule, the ornate ceiling-rose badged with flower heads, grapes, two cherubs with distended stomachs. The porter turned and pointed towards double doors, panes of smoked glass stencilled with a Latin motto, rain darkening the words. Charles thought of the glass plates he was shown in his first term at Cambridge. Images of misshapen and hydro-cephalic skulls. Bird and Charles straining to see as the tutor commented briefly on each. And later that term the cabinet cards they passed among each other with their pictures of babies whose concave heads with massive craters and dips, the names of the photographers in gaudy cursive. One contemporary kept an ape foetus in a jar of formaldehyde, the vaguely humanoid head, long tail, one arm across its eyes as if shielding itself from the horrors of the world.

'Sir.'

The porter bowed then lingered as if in hope of receiving some reward for guiding them through the infirmary. Charles walked past him and held the door open for his mother. The air was cool on his nose and lips. He listened to the reassuring clamour of the city, cartwheels, hoof fall, the yelling and screeching of the hawkers and match girls.

'Mama,' Charles said, 'this way.'

Charles's mother insisted on leaving the window open. He watched the rain falling on her skirt. She unscrewed a perfume bottle and tipped it to her wrist. The scent filled the interior like smoke; small stones thrown by the horse's hooves struck the underside of the cab.

They passed a row of warehouses, their bricks ochre and mole and dark heather, blurring at the window of the hansom. The cab was forced to halt outside the largest one. Vast as a cathedral, as an ocean liner, a facade better suited to a grand hotel in some imperial capital than this enormous showroom for textiles.

As they moved off, to escape the smallness of the silent cab, the air hung with a pungency Charles felt as a pressure behind his eyes, he thought of the city, all the labour in its wards: the calico manufacturers, coopers, cotton spinners, the coal and coke merchants, the importers of ebonite and earthenware, men who sold gauge glass and German silver, makers of hinges and screws, dynamos, driving rope. The hosts of clerks and cashiers, wire workers, wood carvers, spinners of worsted yarn. All living now in this smoke-racked city, lives indivisible from their labour; scraping, cutting, scratching, hammering at their meagre or immodest livings, for it seemed only to allow the two.

Workers were passing through the high iron hoop of the gates of a lamp-wick factory, spilling onto the pavement.

The cab slowed as a handcart piled with firewood was hauled out of a side street. It inched ahead of them. The men pulling ignored the cabman's shouts for them to move aside. Tired of idling behind the handcart the cabman turned down Aytoun Street where a line of boys dressed like medieval friars were being led along by their master from the music school.

Charles watched as the city faded, the architecture dwindling in scale and ambition until the buildings receded to tightly packed rows, gable ends painted with advertisements in wide white letters: ales, hardware, properties for hire. Still his mother remained silent. As they passed the park it began to hail. He watched the pedestrians with their black umbrellas taking shelter in the bandstand.

When the cab arrived at the house he offered his hand to his mother. Clutching the umbrella, his movements were awkward as he engineered her descent from the folding steps. He paid the driver then unlatched the gate, and his mother without looking at him said:

'I spoke with Dr Calthorpe about the child.' She paused. 'No damage he could detect has been done.'

When no response was forthcoming she sniffed then turned sharply, calling out to her dogs who came haring down the path towards her.

December

The trunk was almost full. Charles lowered the lid to test the remaining capacity. One of the ribs had splintered. He ran his fingers along it until they snagged on the broken wood. Had it been like that since Florence? He pictured himself and Bird in a heat-bleached piazza. He saw a shadow grow then recede out on the landing.

'Hello, Tabitha,'

'Charles,' Tabitha said, stepping into the space her shadow had occupied, hands behind her back. 'Mama tells me you are going away.'

'For a short while.'

As Tabitha breathed there was a soft whistling around her nostrils.

'It's not our fault, is it?'

'Not at all.'

'Oh, good.'

She seemed relieved and gave the closed-lipped smile of the habitually praised.

'I thought you might want something to read.'

She handed Charles the *Waverley*, the pages inexpertly glued back to the spine. When she next spoke there was a brittleness to her voice.

'We shall see you again, shan't we?'

'Of course, in no time at all.'

Her face brightened.

'Eloise was awfully worried we should not. I shall tell her right away.'

*

The dining room rose sharply, hung suspended for a moment, then righted itself to the sound of crockery colliding and the muttering of blue-suited stewards.

'I'm informed work is the purpose of your journey?' said Mrs Davenport.

'I intend to take up a position at a cotton brokerage,' said Charles.

He dropped a fragment of bread into his soup and watched it soften and bloat among the strips of carrot and turnip. It was dark at sea, wisps of puce-coloured cloud around the horizon. As the next wave crashed across the bow there was a flash in the far distance, a tinkling and rattling of tableware and chandeliers. Mr Davenport halted a salt cellar with his hand. Age seemed to have claimed his face but left his thick mop of blond hair unaltered since boyhood.

'Wright, I am sure you will have seen Swain Gifford's illustrations in *Picturesque America*. I was one of the original subscribers to the Appleton Edition. Richmond is captured in every detail imaginable, right down to what they term the perpetual requiem of the James River. Is that not a lovely phrase, Mrs Wright?'

Hettie nodded and smiled at Mr Davenport. Another big wave slammed at the bow; a moment of uneasy silence followed, then gradually the sound of spoons against the china bowls and muted conversation returned to the saloon.

'Mr Hunnicutt, may I ask what took you to England?' Charles said, looking to their quieter neighbour, avoiding the Davenports. Hunnicutt ignored Charles and supped noisily at his soup, his napkin in a speckled fan across his shirtfront.

'Six months?' Mrs Davenport asked. 'You have been married for six months at the least I should imagine?'

She gave a weak smile, blinking her briefly narrowed eyes.

'Which would make it a spring wedding. Mrs Wright, you must tell me all. I hear lilies are the fashion in England.'

There were flowers on the altar, a host of candles, tapers honeying above the bleached wax. The priest wore a faded cassock. He spoke in a weary staccato, as if he had read the passages several times already that day.

'Therefore marriage is not to be entered into unadvisedly or lightly, but reverently, deliberately, and in accordance with the purposes instituted by God.'

The church door whined at its hinges, a bar of light wavering down the middle, until whoever was at the threshold changed their mind. Hettie held a posy of winter jasmine, hellebore, aconite, plaited at the stems. Above them, a stained-glass Christ on the Cross, light through which hit the strands of hair oiled flat across the priest's scalp. On a pew at the front Charles's mother and father sat a few inches apart like strangers in a station waiting room. The priest read Paul's Epistle to the Ephesians. Charles felt his hot breath against their faces. A bird broke across the highest part of the nave through a gap in the flashing and out into the winter sky.

When the service was over the priest led Charles's father outside. Charles followed a few paces behind. Hoar frost along the pavement, on the sills of the windows, on the brick slopes, tiny crystals in the names cut into the tombstones. At the side of the church the priest pointed out a fallen gargoyle.

'Work of vandals or perhaps some imperfection in the stone. I suspect we shall never know.' He nudged a fragment with his boot. Charles's father looked up at the broken face.

'I'll send a contribution.'

The priest bowed, then made off along the frost-covered pavement, his cassock billowing. Charles watched the choir being led into the church. The choirmaster held the door open, touching each child lightly on the head. A robin landed on the lychgate, ruffled its feathers and terracotta bib into a puffed ball, an inch of earthworm writhing in its tiny, seed-shaped beak.

Mrs Davenport's eyes, fiercely bright, moved from Hettie to Charles.

'I must confess, I did wonder, did I not,' Mrs Davenport said, looking over to her husband, 'why it was you chose to travel now. It was my understanding that most Englishmen wanted their heirs born on native soil. Yours, it seems, may be a Yankee.'

On hearing the word Yankee, Hunnicutt, linings of his loosely pouched eyes the colour of cut watermelon, looked up from his soup, the spoon poised at his lips.

'Why did you choose to travel now, Mr Wright?' Mrs Davenport asked, acid this time. Charles stood and draped his napkin across the back of his chair.

'I hope you will excuse us, Mr Hunnicutt.'

Hunnicutt nodded at his soup and gave a little grunt like a rooting sow.

'Come,' Charles said to Hettie who slowly got to her feet, one hand on the swell of her stomach.

'I hope I have not given offence?' said Mrs Davenport.

'This ship is the offender here,' Mr Davenport pronounced from under his mop of boy's hair. 'Wright is simply a little green about the gills.' He pointed at Charles with the pepperpot. 'Nothing to be ashamed of, happened to me many times as a young man.'

'Your husband is correct.'

'He is very wise,' Mrs Davenport replied.

*

'And you are certain it will reach him?'

'Dolly says so.'

'How does Dolly know?'

'Oh, Tab. She just knows.'

'She might give it to Mama?'

'I shouldn't think so,' Eloise said, enjoying for once being the better-informed sister.

'When the post arrived I asked if there was any news from our brother and Dolly said no and then I said we should like to write him a letter and asked if she knew where we could reach him and Dolly said of course we do, Cook and I are in regular contact, your brother writes near daily, give the letter to us and we shall get it to him in no time at all, shan't we, Cook? And Cook who was folding napkins at the table nodded. And then Dolly said mind it shall cost you, I'm afraid, then she looked over at Cook and Cook gave a sort of smile and Dolly said a shilling and then Cook pinched her lips and looked a little crossly as though Dolly were being unkind and said no, no, no, an ha'penny. And Dolly said yes, I mean an ha'penny. Then before I could say anything Mama walked in carrying that horrid new dog of hers, the fur on its belly all wet, feet scratching away, and asked me what on earth I was doing in the kitchen. When I turned round Dolly had vanished and Cook was on her way to the cold store. That's when I came up here to find you.'

'Well, if you're sure … ' Tabitha said.

'And I have some more news,' Eloise said, rather grandly. 'Mama says he'll be home in a few months, and that we are to be aunts.'

1905

February

A fluted note from the whistle, white sparks where wheels clashed at the tracks, the headlamps cutting cones through fog which had fallen early that morning.

Tabitha caught her reflection in the windows of the lower deck. She felt herself stoop, instinctively, then worried about her hat – the cabochons of coral, the black velvet roses. It had seemed the most sober. *A perfectly matronly twenty-five*, Eloise had joked at breakfast, barely glancing from the sketch pad open on her lap. But something in her sister's teasing had stuck. At the last meeting Tabitha had felt overdressed. She had been moved by her hosts' seriousness, their lack of, what was it? Artifice.

She had been walking for some time now. Past the stream of trams with their ghostly adverts for Oxo and Ogden's Cigarettes, the noisy drays covered in waterlogged tarpaulins, their tired-looking nags. She had navigated from memory, away from the windows of drapery and plucked fowls, to this calmer district of banks and municipal offices.

She took three paces back and glanced round the corner. Even that looked different from this angle. She was lost, she realised. She would have to retrace her steps. If she could fail in something as simple as changing trams she wondered what else she might offer the world. She felt a sharp tap on her shoulder, then the blood rising in her cheeks.

'Tabitha, what on earth are you doing here?'

'Charles, you gave me such a fright. I might ask you the same.'

He was wearing his felt homburg with its deep blue grosgrain band. A beaver cloth coat, the buttons done up.

'Lunch.'

He placed a hand, which held a lit cigar, on his stomach, pushing it out for emphasis.

'A fatty lamb shank at the Clarendon, to be precise, with a lacemaker from the East Midlands.'

'What did he want?'

'He was looking for an investor to help revive his father's business.'

'Did he have any success?'

'He brought some samples which I thought he handled rather carelessly.'

Charles inspected Tabitha, as if her state of dress might betray her direction of travel.

'Some business with the Ladies' Committee, I suppose?'

His attention was drawn to a man in morning dress with a very hard paunch, making his way towards an oyster bar a few yards from where they stood.

'They want to start paying you a salary, number of hours you give to them.'

He took a puff on his cigar, peering at Tabitha over the pool of blue smoke which struggled to assert itself against the fog.

'What time did Eloise return last night?'

'Around nine. She was at a concert.'

'Or so she says.'

He ran a hand through his beard. It lent him a martial aspect, the look of some prince connected through cousinhood to the late Queen, a minor character in a portrait by Fildes, or so Tabitha and Eloise liked to joke. He had become a little heavier too, this past year.

'And who was that I saw you with last night?' he asked. 'The young woman at the gate. Shawl, clogs, skin like tinned beef, wild mass of hair. How shall I put this – somewhat *distressed*-looking?'

'Oh, that was Miss Kiernan.' Then, gauging she had not quite satisfied her brother's curiosity, 'Eileen Kiernan – she teaches singing at the municipal school. I very much doubt she was wearing clogs.'

'First I find you roaming the city alone, now I discover you are learning to sing. What next? Conducting the Halle?'

'I was returning a pamphlet she had loaned to me.'

Charles pondered this for a moment, inspecting his cigar as if his next quip were written on it.

'"Paris à la Nuit"? "Views of the Danube"? No, something more edifying, I expect.' He tapped a block of ash onto the pavement.

'"Five Nights as a Tramp", whose author, should you care to know, was Anonymous, styling herself simply A Lady. It proffered some quite startling particulars.'

Charles took another puff on his cigar, narrowing his eyes as if Tabitha were very far away and he was struggling to make her out.

'How she had slipped inside one institution carrying only soap, a towel, stockings and a shawl. And while there had consumed tea mixed with plasmon.'

'Sounds rather cosy.'

'Not cosy at all. Not in the slightest,' she said, resorting to the telegraphed style she hoped Charles would take as a cue to desist.

'This business with the Ladies' Committee, I suppose it means you won't be home for supper?'

'I'm afraid there is a small chance I may not.'

Despite his teasing Tabitha felt she could not leave her brother looking troubled.

'Though I shall try my best.'

The look, perhaps Tabitha alone could read, lifted from her brother's face.

'Rotten fog, isn't it?'

'Awful.'

'Which way are you going?' Charles asked. 'I'll escort you.'

*

Georges Verstraeten is the man I love. Eloise scrawled the words in charcoal across her sketchbook. She tore out the sheet, folded it and tucked it into her apron. It felt thrilling to have the words out like that, to think they might be seen by someone here at the School of Art. She had been harbouring the urge to write it all morning, all through the antique drawing class she oversaw – a dozen young ladies squinting at a cracked amphora, rendering it in variously warped perspectives. The drawing studio was empty now, its huge skylights lending an alloyed sense of brightness and gloom to the space below.

On a new page Eloise began to draw Georges from memory. The ridge of his nose. The set of his chin. That dimple – the dimplette. His face, not delicate enough to be conventionally handsome, emerged in just four or five lines. She wondered if she could draw him with her eyes closed. She thought she probably could. They had shared only a few conversations since he arrived in Manchester. She could recall each almost word for word. He had been distracted initially, unsure of her status at the institution, giving her a blunt smile, which did not quite fit his sensual mouth. The second time they had spoken she had asked him about the Académie Colarossi, where he studied under Courtois. He seemed surprised. In conversation with others she had gleaned little bits of information, his father, something in the regional government in Charleroi.

A noise came from behind the glass display cases at the far end of the studio. Eloise turned, leaning to cover the pages of her sketchbook. It was Alexander Broady, one of the school's technicians, a thin, friendly boy, the son of a Methodist minister, with wavy red hair and a sharp jag of Adam's apple. He had clay-coloured eyes, a peculiar pattern of freckling across the bridge of his nose and down his throat. His hands, which he washed more than anyone Eloise had ever met, were red and dry around the nailbeds. He was holding a cane, a prop from one of the drawing classes. Eloise shut her sketchbook with an unintentionally sharp clap.

'He's just back from the continent, you know.' Alexander pulled up two chairs, sitting on one, setting his heels proprietorially on the other. 'Special dispensation from Glazier. Have you ever been to Paris?'

'Once, with my brother, three years ago.'

'Yes, you look the type. Luxembourg, that's as far as I've been. Must cost a bob or two, Paris. Lives in some style, I should imagine, our Monsieur Verstraeten.'

Georges' rooms had been very warm. The smell of cold tea and tobacco cut through with something sharply spiced, a cologne or a pomander at Christmas time. Behind it the vegetative smell of wet plaster. The rooms were on the top floor of a long terrace, a few minutes' walk from the tram stop. They gave the sense he had lived there for a long time. Although this of course could not be the case, as he had only moved to the city less than a year ago. He had been out painting. A set of oilskins lay piled by the door.

'This city has the strangest light,' Georges said, moving a canvas across the room. 'I am painting always at the limit of my … authority,' he said as if he knew it were not quite the right word but was unwilling to waste any longer searching for a better one. 'I think of all my peers I have the most difficult task, redeeming a little beauty from all of this.'

He flicked his brow towards the window and shook his head.

'This morning I spend an hour at Number 8 Dock where I watched them unload a cargo of Australian wool. For what?'

He shrugged at the canvas, its mauves and blues, its patterns of weak light; there was a note of accusation in his voice, as if Eloise had been complicit in bringing him to the city. She felt a need to compensate, to offer him something towards that store of beauty he prized. But whatever that might be she felt he would reject it. There was nothing she could do and that made him more compelling, more abjectly present in her thoughts. She watched as Georges peeled an orange, breaking the dimpled skin with his thumb, then placing the segments, still covered in spongy pith, one by one into his mouth without offering her any.

'It is time to feed the tortoise,' he said morosely, as he finished his last mouthful of orange. He gestured to the squat black-funnelled stove. 'But really, look.'

On the stove a metal plaque read 'The Tortoise' and promised 'Slow But Sure Combustion'.

'Every day, I must feed this infernal tortoise so my rooms here are habitable.'

He turned and fixed his gaze squarely on Eloise.

'So today I will paint you, yes?'

'Yes.'

He stepped towards her, serious and powerfully close, she could smell old sweat on his skin, tobacco smoke. He reached over and undid the bow in her hair, pulled it until it came loose, then folded the length of damp silk and set it on the table.

'Better.'

He led Eloise to a chair by the window.

'Here, sit.'

The seat was thin, she could feel the frame against her buttocks. She watched as Georges hung an apron over his neck and fastened it tightly at the waist.

'Now we begin, yes?'

She did not know what to say. She folded her hands across her lap and nodded.

'Good.'

She had hoped there might be more of an exchange before he began. Some instruction or direction. But there was none. Through the window she could see a coal barge moving along the canal. The wide boat cutting a wake through the stilled water. Georges brought over an easel, a triangle of plane wood, bolted to a cross-beam. It looked handmade, homemade. The wood flecked with cobalt blues and turquoises, colours of a warm south, places of pines and sea breezes, and Eloise could not say if these traces brightened his room or made the place sadder by summoning what was absent.

Behind a thin partition, the end of a brass bedstead was visible. On the sideboard some brown bottles, all empty. A primitive-looking sink containing both cups and unwashed painting apparatus; jars of clouded water. On the shelf above were bird skulls. Tiny, fragile things bleached very white. Their long beaks like little Venetian doctors' masks.

After an hour of concentrated work Georges paused, then lit a briar pipe, studying his sketch then Eloise. He was troubled by one; Eloise could not tell which. She had begun to feel faint, from the fumes of the strong tobacco and the heat off the Tortoise, which he had twice broken from working to feed.

'I think we are perhaps finished for the day,' Georges said, addressing the sketch.

He glanced across to her and offered the perfunctory smile.

'Thank you for agreeing to sit.' He dipped his chin like a spoiled child drilled in good manners then began working his thumb at the metal surround of the pipe bowl which had begun to lift away.

'You perhaps will return, next week. I might continue?'

Working on the pipe seemed to bring him more satisfaction than anything in the last hour.

'I'm sure that can be arranged.'

'Very well,' Georges said, passing the folded ribbon back to her. It had dried out in the hour she had sat for him. It felt brittle, much lighter than when he had taken it from her hair.

'Yes, he does, or perhaps he doesn't. So hard to tell, isn't it?' Eloise said to Alexander Broady.

'Will you be auditioning for our Easter show?'

'I didn't know there was one,' said Eloise.

'Even Glazier gets involved. Last year I played Feste.'

He waited as if expecting Eloise to compliment him.

'I think his soul is in hell, madonna!' he exclaimed, standing and kicking away the chair his feet had been resting on. 'Make me a willow cabin at your gate! And call upon my soul within the house!'

He reached for the cane and raised it as he declaimed.

'I never did work out what a pia mater was, let alone a weak one.'

A short man in a buff-coloured coat leaned around the door at the far end of the studio.

'Coming,' Alexander called out.

He affected to trip, only to recover himself and swing the cane around in his hand.

*

'Well, I believe that concludes our business for this week,' Cecil Ruislip said, removing his spectacles. He was a slight man, with a sparse, neatly trimmed moustache. He looked as if the hour's conversation had exacted a great toll.

'Tell me, Cecil, how's your wife?' Charles pictured a plump woman he had met once in the palm court of the Midland Hotel. Cecil Ruislip simply nodded, then began putting documents into his briefcase, each batch bound in a lurid pink ribbon.

'Do you have plans for the weekend?' Charles leaned back, determined for once to draw Cecil Ruislip into a less formal exchange. He glanced to the courtyard below, a barrow of raw cotton was being pulled across the wet cobbles.

'We are taking an apartment in Lytham St Annes.'

'The crescent is picturesque, I hear, and there's the windmill, of course, not to mention … ' Charles hesitated. ' … the donkeys.'

Cecil Ruislip put on his spectacles. He shook his head. The machines on the floor below moved into a higher gear as he retrieved his bowler from the horns of the hatstand, then raised his briefcase in a sort of sad salute before exiting the room.

*

In the drawer was a letter that had been posted to the office a week ago. Charles touched it then covered it over with a photograph. It had been taken several years ago by a man named Iddon who travelled up to Windermere from Blackpool with his Sanderson Tropical ½ Plate. Seated at its centre was his late mother in her widow's weeds. Her two newest dogs at her feet, a pair of quick-tempered Pekinese pugs, Kreuger and Chun. On her left stood Charles, head angled, squinting slightly; next to him, Tabitha, uncomfortable in her dress; beside her, Eloise. On the chairs to the right of his mother were Claude, in a sailor suit, and Hettie, hands pressed on her lap as if being punished for something. This then was the family. The souls he was bound to; the houses whose upkeep he oversaw; the mills, the various investments the solicitor Cecil Ruislip reported on each week, the inherited dogs. The telephone rang.

'Hello,' Charles said, holding the earpiece an inch from his head, listening to the shrunken voice inside. 'Very good, well, send him up.'

Charles stood, looking down into the courtyard as a trolley of finished bales was wheeled from the building and onto a waiting wagon.

'McDonald,' he said, gesturing to the chair Cecil Ruislip had recently vacated.

McDonald, a former subaltern in the Black Watch, took care of the day-to-day running of the businesses. Charles had asked him to accompany him to Zurich last year. McDonald had dressed for winter, not the stifling

May heat that pursued them across the continent. It had become a running joke, McDonald carrying his greatcoat from place to place. The Tonhalle, its glass chandeliers, high ceilings full of ornate plasterwork, was a strange context for Mr Macara, the President of the British Federation of Master Cotton Spinners, to deliver his paper on 'Organisation'. Charles thought it a bewilderingly open-ended term. Onstage Macara was accompanied by a Bavarian and a Frenchman named Motte. Bon Motte, Charles christened him. 'You know Brahms played here,' Charles whispered to McDonald, greatcoat like a blanket across his lap. 'I've no idea who you're talking about, sir,' McDonald replied. 'One of those chaps up there on the stage, is he?'

That afternoon Charles instructed McDonald to go on to the conference without him. He had wandered around Zurich, looking at the Haus Mercatorium and the Bahnhofstrasse. It had been too hot and he had begun to regret travelling all this way. It was in the lobby of the hotel he first saw her. She was standing beside a palm, holding a rolled-up parasol. She was talking to a porter in a vague, hesitant German which the porter was struggling to understand.

'Might I be of some assistance?'

The woman turned and looked at Charles.

'I'm afraid I'm having a rather difficult time explaining where exactly I would like our luggage taken. There's been some confusion, you see, over the rooms.'

The uniformed porter, blond with blotchy, roseate skin, stared on blankly.

'I've come from Paris, my husband is here speaking at the conference over at the Tonhalle.'

She paused to make sure Charles was taking all this in.

'I've looked at the rooms and they won't do. Now I've spoken with the concierge, who as it happens has very good English, and he has arranged to have us moved to a suite with a more picturesque aspect. However, this young man seems to require word from the concierge before he is willing to move our cases.'

Charles glanced to the trunks a few paces away, enough for a theatre troupe.

'And to compound the situation,' the woman continued, 'said concierge is now nowhere to be seen.'

She looked suddenly very tired and exasperated. There were two children standing by the trunks, a boy of seven or eight and a girl a year or so older.

'I fear my German is only a little better,' Charles said, 'but let me see if I can't intercede.'

He turned and instructed the porter to take the trunks directly to the suite as the lady had requested, pausing only to ask the number of the room. The porter picked up the smaller cases and made his way to the stairs, at which point, the concierge arrived with a glaring look and a formal bow for the woman with the rolled-up parasol.

'Gosh, that seemed to do the trick.' The woman smiled, then offered Charles her hand. 'Beatriz Margosian. And these,' she said, glancing around her, 'are little Leon and Zabelle.'

They sat in wicker chairs by the potted palms. A big mirror behind them, showing the glittering lobby, surfaces polished to a high shine, women lingering under its fans before heading into the May heat and the smell of manure in the streets beyond.

'My husband travels much of the year. We are generally in Paris but in winter there's always a spell in Alexandria.'

Charles tried to imagine this woman, her young children and copious luggage moving between their summer and winter residences.

'It is much less *charmant* than it sounds. Darling, stop that,' she said, addressing Leon who was pulling down a palm frond. She turned to a girl in uniform hovering nearby who stepped in and led the boy away.

'Perhaps we might take some tea, Mr Wright? I'm sure my husband would be pleased to make your acquaintance. Or perhaps something a little stronger? I find sometimes that is the only remedy for such intense heat.'

The tea came and was laid in front of them at the table. Charles found he could not stop looking at her. He tried to compose himself on the wicker chair as Beatriz Margosian outlined her life as if they were friends from the cradle suddenly reacquainted.

'I met him on a yacht of all places. It belonged to a nobleman. A Visconti something or other. Have you spent much time on boats, Mr Wright?'

Besides a trip around the Isle of Wight, Charles conceded he had not and somehow this led to Beatriz Margosian telling him about her life as an actress in the brief years between girlhood and meeting her husband. When eventually Margosian arrived he was a short, wide-torsoed man with very sallow skin. He breathed noisily through his mouth. He looked to Charles like a man assembled for manual work, a compact toughness, a well-fed peasant solidity, in a suit of expensive cloth. He took a long, unblinking look at Charles.

'This gentleman was kind enough to help with the room,' Beatriz Margosian said, rising in her seat and presenting Charles. Charles stood and gave a bow.

'You are working for the hotel?' Margosian asked, his voice clipped and slightly uncomprehending.

'Oh no, don't be silly, Mr Wright is attending the conference, like you, darling.'

'Ah,' Margosian said, now placing Charles.

'And what are your reflections?' Margosian asked, carelessly pouring tea for himself. It splashed onto the saucer which he tipped out into one of the palms.

'Well,' Charles said, 'it seems a long way to come to hear ideas I've heard a thousand times before at my club.'

The pinprick of pomposity seemed to amuse Margosian.

'And at this time of year,' he said, fanning himself.

'Quite,' said Charles, glancing at Beatriz Margosian, who was laughing.

'Well, I hope to see you again, perhaps at the conference?' Margosian said, a slight narrowing of his eyes in what was not quite approval. 'If you will excuse me, I've a meeting to attend.'

McDonald had reported back that evening with copiously transcribed notes as they drank strong beer and ate medallions of pork in a coolish cellar restaurant. Charles's appetite for the conference was even duller the next day. He sent McDonald for the morning session but promised him the afternoon off. Charles wandered down to the park in front of the hotel. He walked around the boating pond. A white-sailed skiff with two children on board was tacking in a slow progress across the water. It was here he saw Beatriz Margosian for a second time. She was alone, the nanny and Leon and Zabelle nowhere to be seen. She wore a straw hat with ostrich plumes.

'Mrs Margosian.'

'Ah,' she said, shielding her eyes from the sun. 'Mr Wright. Playing truant, are we? Soon you will find yourself in possession of *une mauvaise réputation*.'

They strolled around the pond, the park, talking idly of the weather, the suite to which she had been moved, about Beatriz Margosian's life on the stage, her debut at the Haymarket aged fifteen. When Charles enquired about her early life she told him a sequence of conflicting stories:

she was the eldest daughter of a tea planter in Assam, or an orphan raised by Ursuline nuns, or the tenth child of an analytical chemist. She glanced at the clock on the tea house across the pond, took a quick breath as if remembering some important engagement, then, taking her leave of him, said, 'I shall allow you to choose whichever you think best fits.' Charles watched her walk away, no longer in a rush, batting the grass with her parasol.

That evening Charles went down to the lobby of the hotel, to the same table under the palms in the hope he might see Beatriz again. He ordered a brandy and soda which came at room temperature in a tiny glass. When eventually he saw Beatriz she was dressed for dinner, grey silk, patterned with Venetian lace and gold thread. Her hair was pinned, as if she had stepped from the pages of *Paris Temps*. There were diamonds at her ears. She saw him at the table.

'I have enjoyed our conversations. I am intrigued by you.'

She let the words hang in the air.

'My husband will be down in a moment,' she said, handing him the corner of a bill of sale from a jeweller's; on the back was an address in Paris.

'A friend. Write to me here.'

Charles looked up from his desk to hear McDonald finishing his account of the week across the mills. He thanked him for his report, asked a couple of questions to which they both already knew the answer, then walked him to the door. Once again the thought occurred to him that the business was like a stone rolling down a hill; all he need do was not attempt to arrest its progress. When he returned to his desk he made a note that he must not entertain Ruislip and McDonald on the same day again. He opened the drawer, slid the photograph to one side and touched at the letter. There was a knock. He shut the drawer and locked it.

'Come,' he called out against the din of the machines. It was Henry Allsop, the office boy, who ran messages between the clerks and typists two floors below.

'Mr Wright, sir,' he said. 'Your wife is here to see you. Says it's urgent.'

Before he could rise to greet her, Hettie began her monologue, as though they had been deep in conversation only moments before.

'And you see, the thing is,' she said, one hand briefly on her hip, then against her brow as if taking her own temperature, 'I had told the men at Pauldens they were to deliver it today, this morning, before midday, and not, and I expressly said this, not tomorrow.'

The hem of her dress was wet. Her bony, fluent hands moved continually as she spoke.

'I see.'

'No, you don't see, Charles, do you? I said today.'

'Hettie, sit down please.'

'We need this addressed at once. You will accompany me to Pauldens?'

'Hettie, it's the middle of the day, there are four hundred people at work in this building, I am not at liberty to accompany you anywhere.'

Charles gestured to the chair opposite his desk

'Please, Hettie, come on now.'

*

The mother in her high-backed chair looked stately and ancient. Her still, impassive face like a sultan, opulent in the light from the open range. She must have heard many words like these, oratory, impassioned speeches. Perhaps, Tabitha thought, that was why she allowed her young companions to keep talking, to let the conversation spend itself and peter out. Or perhaps she was intrigued by what was being mooted, the spirit with which they held forth, though her countenance betrayed none of this.

'We are talking about taking some form of direct action,' said a woman.

'About bloody doing something,' came a sterner voice from the back of the room.

The mood had changed, the buzz of conversation faded. Tabitha saw the women in the kitchen glance from one to the other, a shifting and settling of skirts. She knew most by sight but only a few by name. There was Eileen Kiernan and her friend Molly Allen. Their hosts, the mother and her daughters who had done so much for the cause. The elder daughter, at the first meeting she had come to with Eileen, had asked about her volunteering at the school, then where her family made their money. She knew of her brother she said, and the phrase had been weighted to suggest something unscrupulous about him, something not beyond reproach. Tabitha had almost risen to his defence. Though what was she being asked to defend? And what did this woman know of Charles?

The younger daughter bent to the range and placed some coal inside. When she looked up her face had reddened. She straightened a brooch on her blouse. The talk of direct action had ameliorated and now a more recognisable set of speeches began; reports, news, letters from friends in London. When the time came Eileen took to her feet, as prompted. She seemed at her most confident among the other women. There was nothing of the circumspect girl she knew from the school.

'It is my belief that the newspapers have begun to lose interest. That we are beset on all sides, despite our best efforts, by inertia and conventionalism.'

A crackle of laughter moved through the women.

'I am minded to return to our founding belief. I echo the sentiments of moments ago: the time for fine words has passed.'

One by one the women bid farewell and left the kitchen.

'A word, if I may.' Her voice was resonant but weary.

'Yes, of course,' said Tabitha.

She patted the chair beside her at the range. There was something slightly sad, Tabitha observed, but also very dignified about her face close up; the long slit of her mouth, the long nose, those wide impassive eyes which spoke both of forbearance and having looked on injustices too long.

'We are grateful you joined us today.'

'I am grateful for the opportunity.'

'There are, to say the least, some testing times ahead.'

A daughter appeared at the door but was waved away.

'Tell me,' she said, leaning forward slightly and taking one of Tabitha's hands in her own, 'what do you make of our Miss Kiernan?'

Tabitha thought about it, not wanting to betray her friend, yet wanting to mark herself out as beyond the normal measure of usefulness.

'She is committed. Intelligent. She burns with an uncommon zeal.'

'And you trust her?'

She was surprised by her host's directness.

'Yes, I do.'

'She is not, how should I put this, too wild? Too headstrong? Too rash in ways which might hamper our efforts? I ask you as a newcomer, as a fresh pair of eyes.'

Tabitha looked into the range as the coals shifted, then up to the cool porcelain of the plates on the dresser.

'If I may speak freely,' Tabitha said, 'I believe Miss Kiernan possesses the exact fire our cause demands.'

The mother took a moment to absorb this, as if filing the words away somewhere.

'Very good, then we are in accord,' she said, and Tabitha's sense of being interrogated lifted.

'I look forward to talking at greater length.' She released Tabitha's hand. 'But for now there are more pressing concerns.' She nodded to her daughter who was standing at the doorway, an empty moleskin coat held up by the shoulders.

'*Jevan, the Prodigal Son* at the Queen's – we've seats in the dress circle.'

*

Dinner on Friday was served at seven o'clock and it had become an unspoken rule that all would attend. There were vases of cut flowers on the table. The electric lights were off, the room lit by palmatine candles.

'She is a dissident, frater,' Eloise said with a smile, 'hatching to bring the whole establishment down. Isn't that right, Tab?'

'Don't be so silly,' Tabitha said, pouring herself a glass of water.

'It's true, I know what goes on at those meetings.'

Eloise glanced to her brother to see if her baiting of Tabitha was amusing him.

'I think the Ladies' Committee has more to do with charitable works, et cetera.' He gave a soft, forgiving smile which seemed to suggest Eloise should desist.

'All that seditious literature on her nightstand. What's his name, Perkin Gilsman?'

'You might want to look inside a book sometime, Ellie, it's a wonder what ends up in there,' Tabitha said drily, provoking a smile from their brother.

'Where's that soup?' asked Charles.

The soup, a *purée de pommes Portugaise*, was brought in by one of the young men who assisted Cook. When first asked, in vague terms, if she might be able to prepare 'more complex dishes of foreign provenance', she had looked at Charles as if asked to dig a privy. The compromise had been an extra pair of hands called in each Friday to undertake the finer work. After soup, there would usually follow a quenelle or a rissole, then beef or medallions of veal, and to finish a milky blancmange or an ice pudding in a fluted pillar mould.

'Well, frater, what do we have from that kitchen of yours today? I must say I was very disappointed we were not joined by another of your guests.'

'Yes,' Tabitha added, 'we should like to have seen more of your Mr Allardyce.'

Allardyce was a barrister with a collection of two hundred South American moths who was writing a paper for the forthcoming volume of the *Entomologist*. After dinner last month he had played a piece from a concerto by a Russian named Goedicke. As he finished he stood up as if too deeply moved to continue with the evening. It was raining heavily and he left without his umbrella.

'I say, do we know if Mr Allardyce made it back to his lodgings?' Eloise asked.

'He really is a remarkable chap,' said Charles. 'I spent an evening with him once at my club.'

'Before he vanished,' said Eloise.

'Quite,' said Charles. 'He listed the names of over one hundred species of butterfly native to England.'

'How many can you remember?' asked Tabitha.

'Let me see,' said Charles, 'setting aside those we all know, the Red Admirables and Painted Ladies, I would begin with the Swallowtail and Grizzled Skipper.'

'We shall need their Latin names,' said Tabitha.

'Well, there's also, the –'

But before he could continue Charles was interrupted.

'Charles, may I speak with you?' Hettie was at the door. She looked pale and addressed the floor. Charles excused himself and pressed his napkin to his lips.

'What is it now?' said Tabitha.

'I've no idea,' said Eloise.

When Charles came back into the room he unfolded his napkin and made to sit down, then pinched the bridge of his nose. He stood with one arm supporting him against the table. His outline looked, to Eloise, like a reaper on a weathervane. He glanced out of the window then exhaled.

'I'm afraid I have a terrible headache, will you excuse me?'

'Charles, don't be silly, of course.'

'Yes,' said Eloise, 'more for us.' She held her knife and fork at right angles to the table. Charles pinched the bridge of his nose again and gave a nod to each of his sisters.

April

Charles was standing in the hallway with Claude, who was dressed identically to his father in a belted Norfolk jacket, bow tie, plus fours and flat cap. Charles had made a promise to Hettie that morning to present Claude at the Royal Windermere Yacht Club. This was met first with enthusiasm from his son, naming the racing yachts they had seen when last there, *Zika*, *Ripple* and *Caress*, which Percy Crossley had let them inspect at close quarters at the chandler's. But over the course of the morning this turned into anxiety, Claude asking who he would have to meet and talk with, about what questions he might expect and what answers he might give. Charles was attempting to find some useful duty for Claude when Tabitha approached them.

'Charles, I've sent a telegram to Knowles and he's made provision for me to return to Manchester on Thursday morning.'

'Thursday morning?' Charles asked, turning Claude by his shoulders and pointing him towards a suitcase at the top of the stairs beside two pigskin hat boxes.

'I have an engagement I cannot miss.'

'May I ask what this engagement is?'

'It is a committee meeting, Charles.'

He mimed thinking, tapping his finger against the bow of his lips.

'The Temperance League? The Manchester Automobile Club?' He laughed then became more serious. 'But you will be returning that evening?'

'No, I will not. My meeting is in the late afternoon and, as you know, it's too far to come up and down in a day.'

There was a peace lily in a metal bowl on the table. He took one of the leaves in his fingers and inspected it.

'Then perhaps on the Friday you will rejoin us?'

'Yes, perhaps on the Friday.'

Tabitha picked up a bundle of clothes she was taking to Windermere.

'You know, I was speaking with Miss Kiernan.'

Something in Tabitha's voice set Charles on edge.

'Did you know every Monday her mother has to pawn the bedding they sleep on.' She raised her bundle for emphasis.

'Are they not in work?'

'Yes, Charles, they are in work and Miss Kiernan contributes her wages to the household.'

'But they are not employed by us?'

'No, Charles, they are not.'

'Then I'm afraid there is very little I can do.'

'Your friends in London, who invest money up here, do they know the effect on humanity or do they think us some wild place?'

There was a pause. Charles seemed to debate whether it was worth responding.

'This –' he traced a loose halo with his finger – 'where do you think it all comes from?'

It was a controlled anger, which sought to relegate this conversation to a place it would rarely be revived.

'Avail yourself of Mr Kiernan one evening,' he continued. 'If you do not find him at home I should think you may at the following: the Three Crowns, the Nag's Head or the Paganini Tavern. And, Tabitha,' he said, hitting all three syllables of her name, as if it were a foreign word she insisted for no good reason on being called by, 'you may be surprised to learn these are not charitable institutions but public houses where, I'll wager, a good deal of Mr Kiernan's income is deposited by his own free will.'

'Hopeless,' said Tabitha.

'And before you ask –' his tone had cooled – 'the workers at all three mills, those at the warehouse on Danzic Street, those involved with domestic and foreign sales, are paid a fair wage. They are not serfs toiling on allotment land, they are, in fact, free to come or go as they please, to seek work elsewhere, and free, as I think it probably the case with your Mr Kiernan, to spend their income in any manner they wish.'

'I was simply appealing to a humanity I know, being your sister and not your employee, has not been completely effaced by your time in business.'

Tabitha knew she should have resisted those final words, she felt it in her stomach, and saw now it had ignited something in Charles.

'When Arthur Holt, overlooker at the mill in Stalybridge, was diagnosed with miliary tuberculosis, we kept him on at a cost of three pounds nine shillings and sixpence per week for four and a half years. When the case for the closure of the mill in Ancoats was suggested I elected not to, compelled as I was by figures set before me both by Cecil Ruislip and independently by a firm of accountants here in the city.'

'Charles.'

He held up a finger.

'There are matters, Tabitha, beyond your high ideals which I beg you leave to those with some experience of the world. I am not your father and I think it marvellous you have received such a fine education, but let me make this clear, there is a gulf between the ideals which you and those leisured women friends –'

'They are not –'

'Please, if you will allow me to continue.' He raised his finger again. 'Between the ideals which you and your leisured women friends expound and real lived experience of the world. Now if you will excuse me I need to finish packing as I believe our train leaves with or without us in one and a half hours' time.'

*

The breeze coming off the lake carried the scent of the cut grass. The train had been delayed at Kendal. They had eaten egg-and-caper sandwiches and played gin rummy in the warm carriage. Even Hettie played a hand before announcing she was too tired to continue. When they arrived at the house Tabitha went room to room directing Knowles in lighting the fires. The dust sheets were still over the furniture from their last visit in the summer.

'Right, who is going to join me?' Eloise was standing in the stone hall. She had her bathing suit on, a blue towel across her shoulder.

'Ellie, really?' said Tabitha.

'Are you going to join us, Claude?' Eloise asked.

'Oh –' he looked surprised at being addressed and involved in something not entirely proper – 'no, I don't think I shall.'

Charles was guiding Knowles as he carried one of the trunks which had been sent up from the station. 'Go ahead, Claude, it will do you good.'

They set off down the sloping lawn and out across the long grass, through the loose clouds of midges that hung a few yards from the shore. Claude was tentative until his aunts, out in the lake to their waists, beckoned him to join them. He stepped to his ankles, the water shimmering around his pale feet, wading gingerly, pushing his hips as if the movement required the greatest effort. When the water reached his belly he stopped and shook his head.

'I'm very sorry, Aunt Tabitha, Aunt Eloise, I can't.'

He turned and waded out, shook himself off, walked quickly to the long grass and then broke into a clumsy, lolloping run back to the house.

'Leave him, Tab, he'll be fine.'

Tabitha, who had followed Claude from the water, stood on the shore. Eloise swam back in now too. She stumbled as she picked her way across the rocks. On the far side of the lake someone had lit a bonfire, a flicker of orange in the distance, behind it the inky outline of the mountains where the light had yet to fail.

'Oh, for the love of God, Ellie, what are you doing?'

'I am being free.' She let fall her bathing costume; it lay crumpled at her feet. She covered her small, pale breasts with her hands, turned and walked into the water until it was over her ankles then her mottled thighs. She breathed out, short tight breaths, as she launched into a stroke that seemed to snatch a little against the cold. Tabitha picked up her costume, shaking the small stones from it.

'Join me,' Eloise called as she rolled onto her back.

'I shall not.'

'It's heavenly without all that garb.'

Eloise was propelling herself backwards, hair floating in a tangled mass around her. The cloud had broken, a long spray of stars visible. Tabitha looked back to the house. There were lights on in the top rooms, a figure moving between the windows.

'You do know Knowles is out fishing tonight. If the pike don't catch you, I suspect he will.'

Eloise cast up her hands, sending plumes of water back towards the shore. They fell short, splashing a few yards from where Tabitha stood.

'There are eels in there, you know, Eloise, huge, prehistoric things.'

Tabitha was tired of waiting; she walked into the long grass, following the path Claude had cut as he ran back to the house. She turned and saw Eloise gliding backwards towards where the moon lay faintly wavering on the water.

'Your costume is on the tree,' Tabitha called through cupped hands. 'Remember, Knowles is abroad, the eels are hungry.'

She was answered by another ragged plume spending itself on the lake.

*

'Claude, tell me, did you swim last night?'

'No, well, a little, I suppose.'

'I thought we might take the boat out today for a sail.'

Claude looked out of the window, making a very careful assessment of the weather. A few drops of rain fell against the glass.

'Is it not a little breezy out there today, sir?'

'I should say it's perfect.' Charles folded his newspaper and placed it on the table. 'If we leave now we can be away before the others come down.'

The leaving without the permission of his mother seemed to worry Claude.

'Sir, if I may, please may I take some breakfast first?'

Charles looked down the length of the boat; the jib was beginning to slap in the breeze. He pulled on a rope and the noise died down, as the boat surged, the power now in its sails.

'A little cold perhaps still.'

'Yes, sir, and I should think quite dangerous.'

Claude gripped the edge of the boat, glancing to his father. He looked worried as another wave punched across the bow.

'Do you see that little spit of land in the distance?' Charles said. Claude leaned back so his head was outside the boat, his hands gripping so tightly his knuckles whitened. When he had seen the landfall he drew himself back in. 'Well, that is our destination.'

Claude nodded.

'How long do you think it will take?' Charles asked.

'I'm not sure, sir, an hour perhaps?' Claude ventured.

'Oh, less than that I should think with the wind behind us.'

The spit of land they were sailing towards gradually revealed itself to be an island. When they reached the shore Charles jumped down and hauled the boat onto the shingle. He offered a hand to Claude.

'Shall we explore? When I was young we would come and search for hours through these woods. I remember a rat scuttling out just over there. One summer we built the most magnificent tree house. I wonder if it's still standing.'

'I think, sir, I would rather remain here on board.'

'Well, I'm going for a wander.' There were fractals of light falling across Claude's face. 'Should I not return within the hour I trust you will do all you can to look after your mother and your aunts. Adieu,' Charles said, walking into the island, trampling down the tall ferns. A few yards into the wood he heard the sound of Claude, clambering over the gunwale, his feet on the shingle then crunching through the undergrowth behind him.

'Pa, please wait, I think I shall come and explore a little after all.'

They were sailing back to the boathouse when the weather began to change. The brightness suddenly sapped from the day, a noticeable drop in temperature. Sets of choppy waves coming across the lake, breaking with a hard slap against the bow.

'Absolutely nothing to worry about, Claude,' Charles said. He was having to concentrate, the wind had changed direction again. 'We shall have to tack to get back in good time. When I say lee ho, you are to release that rope there to your right. Do you see?'

Claude nodded, then looked out across the lake. A pleasure steamer was moving in the direction of a distant pavilion.

Charles was untangling a mass of ropes from his feet. It had begun to rain, wide drops slapping onto the seats, then a finer shower drumming the mainsail.

'Claude, you see the jib is stuck there?' Charles was having to shout against the wind. 'I need you to take the tiller while I release it. Can you do that for me?'

Claude nodded.

'Come here then.'

Very tentatively, keeping both hands in contact with the boat, Claude slid towards his father.

'Here, just keep her steady. I won't be a tick.'

Claude took the tiller and Charles held his hand on it, setting the boat towards the shore. He watched as his father staggered towards the prow.

'Keep her steady,' Charles called back but Claude's attention had drifted, a bird circling on a thermal above. For a moment he let go of the tiller and brought his hands together, blowing on them for warmth. The boat rocked violently. Charles began to fall. He stretched out his arm and caught a handful of the sail with a ripping sound high up in the cloth. He hung over the water then was tossed back into the boat by another wave.

'Damn your eyes, Claude, I said keep her steady.'

Charles clutched the bunched sail; a big tear was visible, a section of grey sky through the slapping cloth. He staggered back and pushed Claude from the tiller.

'Look –' he tried to hold back his anger – 'you did very well there.'

He watched Claude shuffle to his previous position. The wind was up and he was having to raise his voice to make himself heard. 'We're going to have to tack again, do you recall what I told you?'

Claude nodded.

'Good. On my signal release the rope.'

Claude released the rope which hissed through the cleat. Charles ducked as the boom swung round. Seeing his father drop his head, Claude lowered his own a fraction. Charles heard a dull thud, then the wooden mast catching. The boom as it swung round had struck Claude in the face. When he lifted his head there was blood pouring from his nose, his nostrils swelling. Charles pulled a handkerchief from his pocket and tossed it to him. It fell into the wet belly of the boat. Claude bent gingerly to retrieve it, holding the handkerchief to his face where the sodden cotton bloomed red.

*

Hettie had been waiting on the pier for an hour. A young man had drowned in the pond near their village when she was a girl. She remembered them trying to bring his body from the water. The poles they used, prodding and pushing the bloated corpse. She felt sure that something like this had happened to Claude, that out there on the lake something had gone terribly wrong. She saw him cold and lifeless, face down in a reed bed. She had been late to breakfast, and, seeing their napkins on the table, had been overcome by the thought. She had run to the boathouse and found it empty. In the distance, across the water, she could hear an orchestra rehearsing at the pavilion, its glass doors open out onto the lake.

A week after Claude was born Charles had taken her to a dance. The Kissimmee Concert Band at the Grand National Hotel. She had not wanted to leave Claude. Charles had insisted. The soprano, white creases in her neck, wore a red gown, and struggled with the high end of the register, her voice fraying into a reedy tremolo. Among the heat of bodies, the susurrus of skirts over the boards, she began to feel faint. She told Charles she needed to rest. At the far side of the room, on a bank of ladderback chairs, a lady was cooling herself with a point de gaze lace fan, the cord and tassel nested in her lap.

'I must confess when I learned an English couple would be among the party this evening I consulted my *Sherwood*,' the lady said, then in a confiding tone, as if they were old friends, 'there is a chapter on How to Treat the English.'

Hettie remembered her soft, slightly down-turned eyes, her gentle, half-mocking tone as she introduced herself as Miss Anderson and explained how, at thirty-five, she was an 'elderly girl' and had given up any hope of marrying, contenting herself with life in her father's house, an engineer who had worked on the Gulf Coast Canal and written a textbook on hydraulic cements with a friend from Westpoint.

'Now,' Miss Anderson said, 'let me see what I can recall from my *Sherwood.*'

She closed her eyes and pressed her forefinger to her lips.

'The English lady always appears in a semi-grand toilette, with open Pompadour corsage and elbow sleeves –' she paused – 'while her daughters are uniformly sleeveless, and, generally, in white dresses, often low-necked in the depth of winter.'

She applauded herself, the patter of hands in their mousquetaire suede gloves. They talked together a while longer then Miss Anderson insisted they join the quadrille that was about to begin.

'I wondered if we might stay on?' Hettie asked in the carriage home that evening.

'How do you mean?'

'For a few weeks.'

'There are dances in England, you realise.' Charles laughed and closed his eyes.

She did not know why she thought of Miss Anderson, even now as she waited on the pier for Charles to return with Claude. She sometimes thought she might write to her care of the Grand National Hotel. What would she say after all this time? How odd it would seem, this missive from a stranger, from a moment in her past. Still, she could not escape the sense that she had missed, or been denied, a friendship, that the friendship of Miss Anderson might have made her altogether someone else.

She remembered how she had asked, 'Shall we take a stroll?' They had been home in England for a week after almost a year in America.

'A stroll?'

Hettie was dressed and standing in the doorway to the study, holding her umbrella.

'I'm sure my sisters can take you, if you require exercise.'

'I am not one of your mother's dogs, Charles.'

'I'm sorry, what did you say?'

'I am not one of your mother's dogs.'

She had come to the study the day after his mother died. Charles sitting at the desk. His mother's two Pekinese, their crushed faces and little pink tongues, panting noisily in a basket on the floor. Charles was staring at them as if they had just disclosed something of enormous importance.

'I am sorry for your loss, Charles.'

He looked up and through her as if she had been addressing someone else, then let his gaze drop to the dogs, as the larger of the two began lapping at its crotch.

On the pier Hettie saw the boat in the distance. She watched as its red sail slowly grew bigger. She could make out the shapes of Charles and Claude. Then she saw Claude was holding something to his face, and which he held up, on seeing her there on the pier, the sodden red cotton snapping in the breeze.

Daylight was fading by the time Charles finally stored the boat.

'My precious, come here.' Hettie had opened her arms wide as Claude had leapt from the boat, with a sure-footedness that had evaded him out on the lake. He had run towards his mother who had wrapped him in her arms, then tipped his head back to the light.

'Reckless, utterly reckless,' she'd said as she brought Claude's head back to its natural position. The blood had dried around his nostrils. There was a small bruise forming under one eye.

'It was just a knock, I think the boy will live.'

Charles had watched them walk away, Claude taking two small steps for each of his mother's strides, which seemed affected, faintly ridiculous. He had abandoned the mooring, pushed the boat from the pier and set a slow course that would take him the whole ten miles along the lake and back, by which time the day was over.

Ordinarily he would have waited for Knowles to help store the boat but he was content to work alone, his trousers soaked to the knee, his feet numb. In a few days he would see Beatriz again. He had received word last week. It would mean remaining in Windermere. He was yet to contrive an excuse plausible enough to keep him away from the city. He reached into the pocket and took out her last letter.

I am sitting by a tall window at a desk that once belonged to Gavril's grandfather. The curtains are pulsing and beyond them I can hear the city beginning to go about its business. I smell sesame and orange water and something slightly fetid. I hear a cockerel and a braying mule. In a moment the muezzin will start and the faithful will make their way to prayer. Hamid is up and banging about. I hear him shuffling from room to room on the floor above. In a while he will arrive with the tea things, his gap-toothed smile. I shall no doubt blanch and attempt to cover what I have written here though he speaks no English. Gavril dined last night with Evelyn Baring, the consul general, and some others. He returned home at close to three, reeking of brandy, claiming to have bought another automobile. There is some scandal brewing up in Cairo over artefacts that have been sold. In a week's

time we leave for Paris. There is another party in May you
must come to if you can ...

Charles folded the letter and put it in his pocket. He would take the long route back, through the woods, past the stand of trees Knowles planted last spring; if there was any light left he would stop and read the letter again.

*

'I have invited a guest.' Eloise placed the morning's mail on the table. She had intercepted the maid on her way into the breakfast room.

'A guest?' Charles said, looking through the letters uninterestedly.

'A Walloon,' said Eloise, taking a seat to Charles's left, giving a clear view down across the lawn onto the lake. The windows threw wavering oblongs of light across the table. She shook out her napkin and draped it across her lap.

'Or a Fleming, never sure which is which.'

'Is this one of your little jokes, Eloise?'

She shook her head.

'Who exactly is this person?'

'A painter.'

Tabitha, who had been pretending not to listen, now joined the conversation.

'And when are we to expect them?'

'He's arriving this afternoon, I've just had word.' Eloise raised the letter like a bidder at the opening of an auction.

'How exactly do you know this man?' Tabitha asked, her breakfast already under way, two boiled eggs, tops hammered off, gold yolks dripping across her plate.

'He is a colleague at the School of Art. I think you'll like him.'
She leaned for the butter dish.

'And?' Charles nudged the conversation going again.

'And he has been in Manchester for almost a year and is yet to see any of the countryside beyond, which seems a shame, don't you think?'

Eloise broke a roll in two, a few copper flakes falling, like bits of beaten metal, on the tablecloth. Tabitha and Charles looked at each other, seeking a signal it was inappropriate this person should join them unannounced. It seemed neither could quite summon a reason.

'I suppose our Belgian will take the Blue Room?' said Tabitha.

'Or Chestnut, we could put him in Chestnut,' said Charles.

'Rather cold in there, rather small, no?'

'I see,' said Charles. 'Where were you thinking?'

'I was thinking Chanticlair,' said Eloise.

'He must be distinguished,' said Tabitha.

'And what,' Charles asked, in a tone one might enquire of a child's doll, 'is the Belgian's name?'

'Georges,' Eloise said plainly, combing the pliant butter into a soft crest then spreading her roll in three diligent strokes.

'Monsieur Georges,' said Tabitha with uncharacteristic exuberance, as if he were a seaside conjuror.

'Monsieur Verstraeten.'

'Verstraeten?' said Tabitha. 'I imagine him a rather distinguished figure, somewhere in his sixth or seventh decade?'

'Oh no, he's younger than that,' said Eloise, taking a bite from her roll and then turning to watch the cloudlets being blown across the lake.

'Younger,' Charles said, 'though he has a family of his own?'

'I don't think he goes in much for that type of thing.'

'Well, I suppose I should inform Mrs Wright.' He curled his lip like a wounded animal as he rose from the table. The sisters sat in silence, each pretending to the other that they were not listening to the voices from the adjoining room.

*

For the past hour, as his father worked through the pile of correspondence deposited with him that morning and a telegram from McDonald regarding the malfunction of a hydraulic press, Claude had been failing to amuse himself. First with a bilbo, the wooden cup and ball now abandoned at his feet, then a tin Pierrot that spun between sticks when squeezed. The figure moving along the avenue of lime trees easily drew Claude's attention away from the toys.

'Papa, there is a vagrant on the drive.'

Charles stood, removing his lap-desk.

'Hello,' Charles called out. 'I take it you are our Monsieur Verstraeten.'

When he was a few yards from the house, the man stopped, set down his suitcase. He leaned back, hands on his waist. Claude had gone in to retrieve his aunts who stood at the door.

'Mr Verstraeten.' Eloise wiped her hands on her apron as she walked out to greet him. 'Pretty, isn't it?' she said, standing beside him.

'I did not know you were a noblewoman,' said Georges.

'It was in my mother's family. They had a sawmill, I think. You'll enjoy the woods; oak, ash, alder, et cetera. Birds too. Full of them. Perfect for *en plein air*.'

Georges took in the neat white house with its glass veranda, the garden with its long sloping lawn, the woods behind, the lake beyond, with a set of small nods like someone who had had something returned to him completely, with no parts missing.

'Well, let's not stand around, I'll show you to your room.'

In the hallway Georges was introduced to Claude who seemed reluctant to shake the stranger's hand but did so when instructed by Tabitha. Hettie, who had been reading in the drawing room, came into the hallway to meet them. She gave a strange, sour sort of curtsy, then excused herself. Soon the whole party save Hettie were trooping upstairs.

'I'm not sure if Eloise has told you but it is one of the oddities of this house that all the rooms have names,' Tabitha said. 'Yours is Chanticlair.'

The bedroom was filled with warm light, the sun catching and spreading across the polished wood. Ignoring the luggage stand, Georges swung his case onto the bedspread. Then, to the surprise of the others, threw himself up rump first, testing the springs with the flats of his hands.

*

'Monsieur Verstraeten really is splendid,' Claude said to his aunt. 'He's shown me how to tie two new knots, and to make a very decent spear out of a stick.'

They were first down to dinner but were soon joined by Tabitha.

'I'm glad you approve,' said Eloise.

'Do you approve of Monsieur Verstraeten, Aunt Tabitha?'

'Approve? I hardly know the man.'

'You sound like Mother,' said Eloise.

'He doesn't look much like a painter,' said Tabitha. 'He could be a ticket collector on the Stockport tram.'

Eventually Charles joined them, then Georges who was wearing ancient-looking evening dress, his hair brushed back in two wings and heavily pomaded. There was no sign of Hettie and after waiting for several minutes Charles decided they would start without her.

'Surely the world cannot possibly run itself?'

'You keep Egypt, France keeps Morocco.'

'But the civilising influence in those regions is –'

'Théophile Delcassé, Lord Landsdowne,' said Georges, 'I think the situation is dogs and monkeys. What's the newspapers' word for it? Peaceful penetration?'

'Pacific,' said Tabitha.

'I think this is another word for conquest.'

Charles refilled Georges' glass and then his own with the fragrant, blood-black wine.

'And tell me, what do you think of Count Tolstoy,' asked Eloise.

'Tabitha here cuts out his letters from the *Manchester Guardian*. Don't you?'

Tabitha shook her head in the manner of one accustomed to having their lesser secrets casually revealed.

'I heard him described by a fellow at my club, who writes for Scott up at the *Guardian*, as the greatest living thinker in Europe,' said Charles with disbelief.

Georges shrugged.

'I am very wary of Tolstoy,' Charles went on. 'He offers a plethora of vapid utopianisms. It's remarkable his views are held in such high regard.'

'My brother has fallen into the habit of writing letters to the editor of the *Guardian*, he signs them "Qui Vive of Manchester",' said Eloise with a giggle.

'Yes, but you must admit,' Charles said, returning unprompted to the earlier conversation, 'the fresh stability offered by the entente is superior to any other form. Take our own family, we have been at the centre of a number of struggles.'

'Charles, you have hardly struggled for anything in your life,' said Tabitha.

'I'll have you know our father was with Cobden the day he met Chevalier.'

'I never understood if Manchesterism were supposed to be good thing,' said Eloise.

'When I was a boy,' Georges said, 'my father was stationed in Liège. When the metalworkers went on strike he took me out to watch the demonstrations; I think he believed exposing his son to such things might inoculate me from the extremes of political temperament.'

Charles nodded in approval.

'My father and I drove out along the Meuse, where I saw a soldier from the garrison beat a man so badly he lost his teeth. I remember he was wearing a piece of saxifrage pinned to the lapel of his coat. When we were returning home we saw a group of workers pull a soldier from his horse then strike him with a hammer. So as I say, dogs and monkeys.'

'I imagine that first soldier was perfectly within his rights to do what he did,' said Charles, looking around for the decanter which someone had removed from the table.

*

The breakfast room was empty. A silver coffee pot cooling on a cork mat. Georges had helped himself and was outside smoking, his cup and saucer balanced on the arm of the bench, his attention fixed on an outbuilding where Knowles stored the hand mower. As Eloise approached, Georges touched his lips, then pointed to the doorway of the outbuilding. Standing beside Georges, Eloise felt on the cusp of something. She felt this was the moment to act; to do something decisive, unequivocal. She picked up Georges' cup and took a sip from it.

'Martinets,' Georges said, glancing at the empty saucer. The pair watched as one, then two swifts fluttered at a hole above the doorway. He reached into his pocket and took out a leather case, three fat cigarettes clasped under a fraying elastic. He offered the open case to Eloise.

'Gosh, no, far too early in the day for me.'

She realised this was the first time she had seen him in a morning light.

'I remember as a girl being saddened when I discovered one would never hear a nightingale north of the River Trent.'

She laughed then leaned across and took Georges' cigarette from him, taking a tiny puff, screwing up her face.

'I made it my business each summer to listen out for them in the woods here in case one had made it. It seemed such a privation.'

The confession seemed to soften Georges, a sense of calm settled between them.

'I thought you spoke very eloquently last night,' Eloise said, passing back the cigarette. 'I'm afraid my brother can be a bit of a bore when he gets going, he's not really stood up to often and, well, it's healthy for him to be reminded there are opinions other than his own in circulation.'

Georges parted his mouth so the smoke hung around his teeth and lower lip, drifting away until he sucked it back in with a hiss.

'And your parents?' he asked, looking around as if he might spot them approaching across the lawn.

'Ah, no longer with us.'

'I am sorry.'

'My father, oh, a decade ago. Mama, suddenly, the year before last. Her heart.' Eloise tapped her breastbone. 'She was sleeping.'

The daring which has risen in Eloise moments earlier suddenly seemed to evaporate.

'I think losing my father changed us all. My brother especially, all that responsibility.'

Georges was looking at her as he did when he had painted her.

'Well,' Eloise continued, 'we're all very pleased to have you here. If that wasn't clear already.'

Georges smiled, showing his teeth, tobacco-stained along their gullies.

'I'm afraid I'm a little chilled. I think I shall go and take some breakfast. Do feel free to join us –' she paused – 'or not, of course, just as you wish.'

She stopped at the doorway and turned.

'I suspect there'll be some kind of activity in the offing after breakfast. Charles doesn't like an idle hour up here.'

*

'As I showed you, Claude.'

Georges raised his voice against the breeze which had begun to stiffen. He lay on a picnic blanket, a paper sack of cherries in front of him; a fire a few feet away had been started from driftwood and dry grass, the flames oily against the daylight.

'Yes, Monsieur Verstraeten.'

Claude cast again, tentatively, following the jangling lure from behind his shoulder and onward as it slapped abjectly into the lake.

'Better.'

Claude wound the lure back in; it skittered across the water. He cast again with more force this time. It floated through the air then fell with a plop into the lake.

'Bravo.'

They had spent a long time selecting the lure from the tackle box that morning. Claude had chosen the largest and ugliest; the size of a stag beetle, six barbed hooks dangling from its belly. They had all been surprised at breakfast when Georges declared he wished to fish, more so when he asked, 'You will join me, Claude?'

Claude, glancing to his mother, had said, 'Yes,' very tentatively.

'What does the lake here hold?' Georges asked Charles.

'Charr, trout. Salmon migrate through every spring. Eels, of course.' Charles ringed his forearm and shook it. 'You know the charr have been there since the Ice Age. Remarkable.'

Eloise brought the back of her hand to her mouth in an exaggerated arc.

'A Holarctic salmonid, which is to say, the fish migrate to sea as juveniles and return to fresh water where they reproduce. I can see I'm boring you, Eloise, but our guest here is interested, I can assure you.'

The tip of Claude's rod was dipping down in little fits and starts.

'Do I have one?' Claude said, glancing quickly over his shoulder to Georges then back to the concentric set of ripples.

'Yes, calm, calm.' Georges got up from the blanket, spat a cherry stone into the grass. He came and stood behind Claude.

'Now, reel.'

The boy's hand moved quickly on the reel, a clacking sound as the line fed through the eyes of the rod.

'Stop. Pull.'

Claude pulled back, the stiff rod creaked.

'Good. Again.'

He did the same and for a moment the fish glinted above the waterline.

An ugly cylinder with a yellow underside and speckled fins lay on the shore stunned, mouth opening and closing as if by clockwork. Its tail fin curled into a sickle, pulsing upwards. Georges knelt down and eased the hook from the fish's mouth, a little puff of blood on the stones.

'And now,' Georges said, handing Claude a rock. 'Once and fast.' He mimed bringing it down. Then gestured to above the eyes.

Claude took the rock and weighed it in his palm, as if unconvinced by its heft.

*

'May I come in?' Charles asked.

Hettie slid the needle into the swell of the pincushion, then placed it inside the open box, beside the reels of thread. It was stuffy in the room, the hot, bottled-up smell of book dust and stagnating water from a vase she had forbidden the maids to change. Charles made his way towards the window where she sat.

'I am going to stay on for a night or so once you leave on Sunday.' He tried to keep a brightness in his voice.

'I see,' Hettie said, as if some previous arrangement was being reneged upon. 'And why, if I may ask, is that?'

She looked down towards the lake. A boat was moving from behind a line of trees on the promontory, a white sail on the dark water.

'Knowles has a few matters he needs me to oversee.' Charles let the half-truth hang for a moment, then sensing it had not quite done its work added, 'The high wall. Some replanting. And there is a wool wholesaler in Carlisle, McDonald is insisting I meet with, something about expanding our lines.'

'I shall need money for the servants.'

'Of course.'

'I hope you don't expect me to supervise the travel of your sisters?'

Charles shook his head. He turned and took her hand which she did not resist.

'Do you remember when Claude was tiny and we brought him here the first time? I was thinking about it this morning.'

'Why must you always talk of the past?'

It was as if a low current of electricity had been run through the room. He would need to be careful. They looked out towards the boat. For a moment there was just the sound of their breathing.

'I know you've been with other women, Charles.'

'I have not been with other women.'

'I know you've been with prostitutes. I have received letters. I have evidence.'

'I have not been with prostitutes.' He was weary and could not disguise it.

'Do you think I don't know, Charles? Do you think I'm an imbecile?'

He sat still and said nothing.

'You are a very cruel and thoughtless man, do you know that?'

*

On the platform the wind was turning over the soil in rain-swollen barrels which in summer months held purple and yellow pansies. Charles looked down the track then checked his watch. He wasn't to meet her at the station, this had been established in a telegram. There was a tea room nearby. She had time between trains. At the far end of the platform, he watched crows circling above the goods yard, where the train lines began to curve towards a stand of tall trees, some bare fields. He felt the cold raw on his face, through the leather of his gloves. He slid his hands into the pockets of his overcoat, stamped his feet, then turned and walked briskly from the platform.

In the tea room Charles found a seat at a table set for four. It was warm inside, the windows blank with condensation. There was a shelf, teapots and Toby jugs with distorted mouths and noses. On each table greasy paper roses in little jars. He watched as a boy wiped his fingers down the window, leaving wide lines under the brass bar, and was scolded by his mother, who pushed him onto his chair and pointed sternly at the soggy slab of raisin bread. Charles watched the boy sullenly tearing a corner, then glancing at the window where the marks had begun to condense, leaving only the faintest trace of his touch.

Charles ordered a pot of tea. The bell at the door rang. An elderly woman with a younger companion in an ill-fitting tweed jacket. A few moments later it rang again – it was the boy who had been playing at the window and his mother leaving, she had lost patience with him. The boy was crying and his mother tugged him by the collar onto the street. The tea arrived, set down unceremoniously by the waitress. Charles looked into the brown pot, the oily sheen on its surface, the leaves black and bloated. He saw the cup and the chipped bowl with the cubes of sugar, then with a flicker of irritation, saw the cup was without milk. He looked up to find the waitress but instead was met by Beatriz, standing at the door.

She was dressed in white and cream, with a high lace collar. Dressed for the date on the calendar and not the state of the weather. She had a white fox fur over her shoulder. Her hair was run through with auburn. He had not noticed this before, not in their hours together in Zurich, not in their single night in Paris.

What else could he remember of that night? He had reconstructed it over and over in the months since. She had known almost everyone at the Moulin de la Galette, leaving him with an elderly senator who pressed his mouth close when he spoke, his sour breath and guttural French, as Beatriz flitted from conversation to conversation. They had eaten oysters, fat oysters coated in a bitter liquid, and then she had taken him in a motor taxi to the Boulevard de Clichy where they were joined, it seemed by prior arrangement, by a man named von Adelshausen. Beatriz introduced him as the Oberst. The lower section of von Adelshausen's cheek bore a series of faintly knotted scars. He accompanied them to supper, where he barely touched his food, then to a hotel where he drank champagne with a measure of gin and a teaspoon of sugar he administered himself carefully as a chemist might some volatile and unstable powder. Von Adelshausen claimed Gavril was a close friend but he was critical of him and spent the early part of the evening complaining about his reluctance to invest in an armaments firm in Essen.

'Simply nothing to him, nothing,' von Adelshausen repeated as he became more drunk, as if Charles might be of influence.

'When we were at the villa in Werfen, last summer, he promised me, he looked me in the eye and said, Audo, I am a man of my word. But now ... ' Von Adelshausen lifted his glass forlornly, which a passing waiter took as a signal for service until von Adelshausen shoved him away, his cheeks a scalded pink. Around midnight von Adelshausen saw a woman he knew, and rising from the table stumbled towards her, leaving Beatriz and Charles alone. They had consumed three bottles of champagne. The entire city seemed to have decanted itself into the hotel bar. A band was playing. Figures in black shifting and swaying. He had kissed her, her mouth was cold, she let him for a moment, then pulled away. Next came their choreographed arrival at Charles's hotel. The sobering lights of the foyer where he feigned reading a newspaper, then followed a minute after he saw her ascending the stairs.

'You have a bath,' Beatriz said, surveying his room.

Charles sat woozily on the edge of the bed. He took a cigarette from his case and lit it. The sound of the faucet, then the smell of some unguent, rose oil, added to the water, came to him, mingled with the smoke. The sound of the water stopped. Beatriz appeared. She was wearing a blue robe, fastened loosely below the line of her breasts. Her body thin, and lithe and hard beneath it. He lay back on the bed. The room had begun to spin. There were prints of birds of the tropics around the walls; spoonbills and cocka-toos and parakeets in neat gold frames. He felt his mouth flood with saliva. The glossy bedspread cold against the tips of his ears. Then the cigarette, suddenly weightless, dropped from his fingers. He had woken the next morning fully clothed. No sign of Beatriz.

*

'Not quite the Hotel Ritz. Not quite Paris,' Charles said, pulling his chair closer to the table with its brown glazed teapot, the jug of milk which had arrived moments before.

'I think it's rather lovely,' Beatriz said, removing the pins from her hat and placing it carefully on the chair beside her. She looked so well Charles thought, so unchallenged by life.

'Rather wicked of me really, alighting here. We are on our way to Scotch-land.'

Charles smiled.

'I am the advance party. Some dreary duke Gavril met last year in Théoule-sur-Mer.'

He wasn't sure if he should stand, if he should lean across the table and greet her with a kiss. He simply sat there as an elderly man at the table beside them stared over at Beatriz. His cheeks were windburned; a pewter moustache drooped over his red mouth. Eventually he turned back to his wife, pushing a piece of pudding across his bowl, his fork scratching the glaze, before lifting it to his mouth.

'Charles, give me your news? Wright & Co., is it thriving?' And then a smile that suggested the whole encounter was a charade. He didn't want to talk about machine tools or cotton tariffs. He wanted to touch her, to reach across and take her hand.

'Leon is growing terribly quickly. He's a little brute. His latest obsession is racing – do you know anything about horses?' Beatriz said, signalling to the waitress for a cup. 'He tells me the best stallions are Arabian, the best mares from Abyssinia. He is taking after his father – some days he even accompanies him to his office.'

The waitress came and set down a second cup and saucer.

'I have a dilemma. Gavril has somehow acquired a chandelier. Hideous, I should add, gaudy, third rate, vulgar.' She spoke as if they were involved in some simple domestic conspiracy, as if they were both Gavril's children. 'I cannot decide on the best course of action. To have this hideous thing hang in our home or to tell Gavril that I simply cannot accept such unnecessary ornament.'

Seeing this had failed to rouse any interest, Beatriz changed the subject.

'Tell me, did you ever buy that motor car?'

'I did, in fact, yes.'

'Gavril seems to be collecting them like marbles. What species is yours?'

'It's an Imperial.'

'I say, that sounds wonderful,' said Beatriz as if it were something deeply illicit. 'Did I tell you about the expedition Gavril undertook? Drove all the way from Istanbul to Marseille, in record time. He would telegram at each stage. We threw some wonderful parties while he was gone. Von Adelshausen was on hand to help. Such a shame you met him when you did, awfully worked up about that arrangement with Gavril, he's still yet to forgive him.'

Charles could feel the conversation escaping him. He felt himself kept artfully at bay. They talked of Alexandria briefly, about her children again.

'Beatriz, there is something I must ask you.'

*

'Oh, Charles.' She looked at him as if he had said something imbecilic for which he could be easily forgiven, a look he suspected usually reserved for Leon and Zabelle.

'But we could … ' He felt his voice waiver, the back of his teeth suddenly very dry. 'Beatriz, I want you to come and live with me.'

'In England? With your wife and child?'

'I have thought of you every day since Zurich.'

She made a shushing sound which seemed to deepen their complicity and yet to dismiss him entirely. He felt his desire reach a new pitch.

'Your letters. Why come all this way? To torment me?'

'Charles –' her voice was tender, plaintive – 'I have Leon and Zabelle, I have Gavril. These are inescapable facts.'

All of a sudden Charles felt very shabby and embarrassed to be there. He could smell his own sweat through his suit. They talked a few minutes more, stilted, polite exchanges, like people introduced only moments ago. Then Beatriz finished her tea, swirled the final sip around her cup, glanced at the clock above the door.

'Will you accompany me to my train? If we leave now I shall be in very good time for my connection.'

*

Charles watched as Beatriz made her way to her compartment. He had half expected her to turn, to offer a wave or a smile; to hand a note to a porter, some scribbled instructions to meet her in Edinburgh or Glasgow or a tiny Highland station where she would be able to see him for an hour. She took the hand of the guard, her boot on the footplate, and stepped into the carriage. She appeared at the window of her compartment, the back of her head to him. She did not move. She must have known he was there, she must have seen him as she took her seat, but as the train blew its whistle, huffed its minerally gouts of steam into the air and began to heave itself away, she sat there motionless.

October

Leaf matter scored a dark line around the skylight. Cloud was being driven by the wind, patches of dappled sun appearing then vanishing on the plaster casts and timber floor. The room had recently emptied of students who had worked there all morning as an obese brunette in a laurel crown moved through a series of poses. Something of their residual heat remained, the air thickened by their collective breath. Eloise was sifting broken pencils from cans that had once contained condensed milk. Alexander sat with a notebook on his knee, the stub of his own pencil – pocked with teeth marks – moving rapidly in his hand. He would pause from time to time and bring a cigarette to his lips.

'Catch you at whatever it is you're up to and Glazier will have you on a charge,' said Eloise. He continued scribbling then pressed the point of his pencil in a full stop.

'That's half the pleasure,' he said, assessing the merit of what he had written.

Eloise came and gently took the notebook from his hands.

'My God, Alexander. You're writing poetry. I didn't think you had it in you.'

When he replied it was coolly.

'I'm fairly good at everything I turn my hand to.'

'Oh, read a little, please do.'

He looked at her in a way that was both shrewd and very simple, like a cattle dealer, appraising both the health of a beast and its value at market. He stood up, and Eloise handed the notebook back to him.

'*A willowed green, an island full of rain, somewhere thunder moving up the river*.' He flashed his eyes from his notebook to Eloise. '*I thought of you, I thought of your soft name, and wandered there a moment without wonder*.'

He seemed suddenly to lose the will to read.

'Marvellous! Will we be seeing an anthology from the Macmillan Company? Covers of green cloth with a crown in gold leaf?'

'I happen to have been in correspondence with Henry Newbolt. Sent him a sheath of verses, he wrote back praising their sonorousness, offered to show them to his publisher, same chaps who did Byron.'

Reading had stirred something in Alexander. He was standing now in the space the life model had occupied earlier.

'Newbolt wrote a cracking poem about cricket.'

He hunched forward, his fingers splayed into claws.

'*There's a breathless hush in the close tonight, / Ten to make and the match to win, / A bumping pitch and a blinding light, / An hour to play and the last man in*.'

He jumped as if startled by something.

'You know I could have played for Lancashire. I was very handy with the bat.' He mimed a defensive stroke. 'But they called me the Devil Himself on account of my bowling.'

He took a measured pace backwards.

'White Coppice First Eleven up at Anglezarke. More wickets the year we won the Palace Shield than anyone in the league. The mill up there was owned by a chap called Eccles, great friend of my father, both Temperance men.'

He affected a look of boredom, his mouth a disdainful moue.

'I was caught taking a crate of ale into the dressing room with Willie Blythe, our wicketkeeper, both of us banned for a year. That was the end of that.'

He took another pace backwards, between two easels.

'My run-up was the key.'

He half jogged, half shuffled towards Eloise, executing a windmill motion with his arms, so quickly it caused her to flinch. He picked up his notebook and the stub of his cigarette.

'Are you still working on those etchings?' he asked, inspecting his cigarette and deciding it was finished.

'Oh, to be frank, I'm feeling a little lost with it all.'

'I thought those nudes were marvellous – I'd some carbide needles I was going to offer you for a very reasonable price.'

'I'm currently working on a portrait of an acquaintance of my brother. A Mr Henthorne. I spend an unchaperoned hour and a half each evening at his chambers. He bought a whole new set of oils for me, Lefranc and Foinet, from Lionel Nathan. Insists I leave it all there; oils, brushes, my apron. Artfully arranged. I think he likes to show them off to visitors.'

Alexander laughed, reaching for the jacket on the back of his chair.

'He insists on wearing a rather gaudy silk tie like some Italian duke. I explained electric light alone was not ideal.'

'What did he say to that?' Alexander asked, pulling a bottle of framboise from his jacket. 'A little contraband from my cycling tour of Luxembourg.'

He unscrewed the top and took a glug of the viscous raspberry liqueur. He passed it to Eloise.

'Henthorne,' she said, licking a drop from her lip, 'told me that I could have as many lamps as I needed, which missed the point somewhat. Charles is awfully impressed by him. Calls it collecting money. What time is it?'

'A quarter to five.'

'Dash, I'm to be at Henthorne's on the stroke of the hour.'

*

Eloise peered round her easel and discovered her subject fast asleep. She observed him for a moment; vulnerable, animal, denuded of his waking prowess; the sclerotic set of the lips, the soft bellows of his breathing. She put down her brush and stood back comparing the sleeper to the figure on her canvas. It was a good likeness. She had been faithful to the strains of grey in his beard, the faint pinkness, purples and carmines around the nostrils, the slight coarsening at the tip of the nose; but it wasn't exact, there was something wrong about the mouth.

She wiped her hands on her apron, leaving silverish smears, that difficult shade of cloth on the lapel of Henthorne's suit. She had been trying to get it right but had given up. She undid her apron and hung it on her easel. Mr Henthorne had begun to snore, sliding forward in his chair. There had been a celebration that afternoon, a festive mood as she entered the chambers, setting down her umbrella and removing her rain-slicked gaberdine, some deal with representatives of a corporation in Hong Kong. Mr Henthorne had offered her a glass of champagne. He had drifted off as she began work, his face moving through a complex set of soft reds.

The door into Henthorne's office was open. Eloise wandered into the brightly lit suite, wood-panelling then tiled to the high ceiling. There was a bowl of Turkish Delight on the desk; she helped herself a cube, its soft perfume growing gluey in her mouth. There was a part-smoked cigar in his ashtray. She held it, light as a piece of a wasp's nest. She wet her finger and rubbed some of the ash into her palm. It was a colour closer to Henthorne's lapel than Lefranc and Foinet had got her all afternoon.

Eloise was glad to have got away early. It was an important night. Ever since Georges' visit to Windermere she had pondered how to proceed. Over the past few days her pondering had resolved itself into a plan, or rather series of impulses she felt duty-bound to follow. She hurried down King Street, the street lamps coming on, the Eagle Insurance Company sign on the metal balcony that ran around the high windows. She recounted all the tiny clues from their conversations – and his coming all the way to Windermere, wasn't that the biggest clue of all?

When she returned home Claude was bidding farewell to his tutor, a wiry man with an ancient pair of pince-nez and a dry cough in the front of his throat.

'Any sign of your aunt, Claude?'

'Oh, no, Aunt Eloise, I think she may be out at one of her meetings.'

'And your papa?'

'He won't be back for hours.'

'Your mama?'

'She's resting.'

Eloise suddenly felt responsible for the boy.

'And you have work and whatnot to be getting along with?'

'Oh yes, Grayson always leaves me plenty.'

*

At the Town Hall there were six speakers facing the audience. A purple cloth with an embroidered coat of arms – a shield of red and gold, a globe covered in bees – was draped over the table. An hour into the meeting and the sense of expectation with which it had opened had dissipated. Each Member of Parliament had made their speech; bloodless addresses on Home Rule and a statement about Shipping Intelligence in the Port of Manchester and the tonnage of cargo through Eastham Locks.

Two of the Members of Parliament had travelled from London, a plump man who was sweating and another with a white moustache who the chairman introduced. There followed a speech on the scarcity of the cotton operative and a claim that all the Lancashire cotton requirements could be grown within the British Empire. The final speaker was talking about electoral reform and the prohibitive cost of elections; he would occasionally bang the table, setting the surface of the water glasses trembling.

'He is saying nothing whatsoever,' Tabitha said to Eileen Kiernan.

Tabitha had watched them assembling the stage earlier. A pair of men in brown coats carrying the table into position, section by section, while another laid out the chairs. She had tried to appear inconspicuous but eventually a clerk, a balding man with a very kind face, approached and asked if he might be of assistance. She had simply said, 'No, thank you,' and hastened from the room. She'd had a story about a cousin she intended to meet but found herself unable to deploy the subterfuge. It had felt like a little defeat, an undoing. She had waited downstairs in the Statue Hall. There was a growing, expectant crowd. She had found Eileen and made a line directly for her. They had filed in with the others.

Now the chairman was nearing the end of his comments. Tabitha felt her heart starting to race. Her palms were clammy and beginning to tingle. She nodded to Eileen. They raised the banner in unison, each moving to the side as it unfurled, then stepped up onto their chairs, Tabitha steadying herself on the shoulder of the man beside her who looked up puzzled then turned away in disgust. They began to chant the slogans they had rehearsed, hissing voices telling them to sit down. Tabitha saw one of the Members of Parliament catch sight of the banner, lean across to the man next to him as if to have him confirm it. His white moustache twitched. The stewards at the front of the meeting began to hurry towards them.

It had taken hours to sew. Eileen had bought the cloth from a shop near her house in Ancoats. They had cut three of the letters and stitched them, deep purple on black sack-cloth, before Tabitha raised the concern that they would simply not be visible from any distance. The pair peered down over the banner, then hung it in the kitchen window and stood at the back of Eileen's yard, the letters hard to see. Eileen sent Tabitha off to buy the new white fabric. The draper's in Ancoats was closed; she had to take an omnibus into the city. It was dark by the time she arrived back at Eileen's.

Tabitha saw Eileen reach into her skirt pocket for something, an egg, bluish and flecked with straw. Eileen hurled it towards the stage. 'Deeds not words,' she said under her breath, throwing a second, then a third which fell short, striking a woman on the front row who let out a yelp, as if scolded, her husband clawing the yolk from her shoulder. This had never been part of the plan. In all the hours of preparation this had never been discussed. A constable was beside the stewards now who were pointing them out.

Tabitha felt a hand on her shoulder. The sense at first of an overwhelming weight which translated itself somewhere in her mind into strength, into force being applied directly to her. As the fingertips dug in behind her collarbone there came a sudden sense of the inescapability of what was happening. The chair being kicked out from under her, the immediate weightlessness, her legs thrown into the air. The strange sight of her boots, her flapping skirt, then the floor rushing up, banging her tail bone, her head whipped back. An ache spreading through her as if she had eaten something far too cold. A series of discrete but somehow interlinked sensations; the weightlessness, the impact, the aching. Down on the floor, there was a ringing in her ears. Noise and commotion all around her. The police officer's helmet had come off. It lay beside her, so close she could smell his unwashed hair. Someone was twisting her arm up her back. Nearby one of the stewards was standing on Eileen. Tabitha watched as she spat at his boots. He bent down and struck her across the mouth with the back of his hand. There was a commotion as the members of the audience turned their attention to the women pinned to the floor. Tabitha saw Eileen's mouth, the blood glossy against her teeth, as she resisted the stewards who were struggling to hold her down. A second constable had joined them. It had all gone wrong. She saw the rage in the eyes of the men above her. Their eyes were bright with it.

*

Eloise inspected herself in the mirror of her mother's dressing table. She had removed the shade from the standard lamp, leaving the bare bulb exposed. The room had been left exactly as it had been before her mother's death, no attempt made to clear any of her possessions; even her bedside reading remained. Tabitha told Eloise it was improper when she suggested they choose some things of hers to keep; Charles was no better, and Hettie had suddenly afforded the space and her late mother-in-law a reverence she had not in life. The accommodations of those first weeks of grief had hardened into routine, into a sense that it was somehow now improper even to enter the room. Eloise had locked the door that led to the wood-panelled hallway that in turn led to the bedroom. It pleased her to be hiding inside her own home. She poured herself more hock into the hollow-ribbed stem of the green wine glass. It was, she supposed, meant to look like something from the Middle Ages. The wine was dry and very acidic. She was learning to enjoy the taste. Forcing herself. That instant uplift of the first few sips was agreeable, but not the ensuing hotness in her cheeks, which made her look clownish, those uneven red lozenges. She inspected herself in the mirror, turning across the light thrown by the bare lamp. She hung a gold locket engraved with forget-me-nots around her neck. Her hair was in a loose coil and she inserted a pin with a crown of rhinestones. She glanced again into the mirror, applied pearl powder. She walked to the bedroom window, pressed her cheek to the cold glass; the rain sounded like young wood on a bonfire. She would be drenched stepping out even as far as the high street where she might flag down a motor taxi. There was only one thing for it ...

At the turn of the stairs Eloise was met by her sister-in-law.

'Where are you going?'

'I've an engagement. Are you on your way to bed?'

'Does Charles know?'

'Yes, absolutely,' she lied.

Hettie looked at her, then placed her hand on the side of Eloise's face.

'You look very pretty.'

Eloise smiled, hoping not to be detained.

'You are so lucky. Do you know that?'

'Yes,' said Eloise. Hettie did not look well. Her skin was almost translucent, she was very dark under her eyes. She was carrying a cup of beef tea, a sharp and sweetly rotting smell.

'So lucky.'

'Thank you.'

In the kitchen Eloise took a candle and a box of matches from a drawer. There was no sign of Dolly or Cook. She carried the candle down into the cellar. At the bottom of the stairs there were shelves, a dozen bottles on each; on the top shelf jeroboams of Bordeaux and a mildewed wicker wine cooler. She took a bottle of Hochheimer and a bottle of port. She wiped the cobwebs from the label, pictured her and Georges sitting before the 'tortoise', the architecture of their conversation, her subtle disclosures, the inevitability of what would follow. She placed the bottles in a laundry bag with a soft clink.

She made her way up a second staircase that connected the cellars to the garage. The steps were cold and smelled of rain. As she neared the top her candle flickered out and she found herself in darkness. She struggled to light another match, the damp heads crumbling on the strike strip. She climbed the stairs into the garage where she threw on the electric light. Everything was made so much more certain by the wine. The world softened, her actions easier and more definitive. It didn't seem to matter what Charles might say if he found her in here, she felt, in fact, he might endorse it. She looked across the garage and there it was, big as a rhinoceros, under the dust sheet.

Charles's gloves and goggles were on the driver's seat. She lit the headlamps, then went to the front and cranked the engine handle. Nothing. She tried again, harder this time, as she had seen Charles do it. He had allowed her to drive it once near Buxton last Whitsuntide. She remembered he had fiddled with some switches by the steering column. She tried a few at random. On the third attempt the vehicle came to life. She opened the garage doors then ran back to the automobile, released the brake and set off into the glittering black night.

She was cautious at first, as she turned onto the street, the Imperial responding to a lighter touch than she remembered. As she drove she felt a thrill, the emissary of her own seduction, past the grand villas then the rows of cheap brick houses, following the tramlines down the unpeopled streets until she could hear the horns and funnels from the docks.

She hadn't thought about stopping. As it dawned on her, she felt a faint sense of panic. Suddenly the automobile that had handled so easily, so naturally, became alien and beyond her control. She glanced around her for the brake, tried to remember what she had seen Charles do. She pulled a lever, the Imperial shuddered but continued moving, she pulled another and it seemed to gain speed. She pulled three in quick succession and it came abruptly to a halt hurling her forward. She scanned the street; there was a grocer's shop and next door to it a stationer's. She must try to remember this, she thought, as she retrieved the laundry bag from the footwell.

*

When Eloise arrived at Georges' rooms she felt a sudden hollowing. The front door was ajar. She let herself in. There was a bicycle in the hallway. Smells of fat and boiled cabbage. She could hear each tread on the bare staircase as she made her way to his rooms, stilling the bottles as their clinking threatened to betray her presence. There was a plaster model of a dancer in a plant pot outside the door. She turned the knob, felt the latch release, pushed it open an inch. There was humming from inside, then laughter.

Georges was standing in the doorway to the bathroom, with its low sink and zinc bath. The tiny window behind him was damp. She could see him in his shaving mirror. His hair was wet, made dark by the water, falling in tendrils around his face. He had a thin towel. She watched for a moment as he tied it around his waist. The fine musculature of his body, like a skinned rabbit, reddened from the bath, his thin slightly bowed legs. She was on the verge of saying his name but instead something made her step into the room.

Lying on the bed was Alexander Broady. He was naked. His face flushed down the bridge of his nose and in wide, uneven patches across his cheeks. His body, ghostly against the quilt. She saw the nest of umber pubic hair, his flaccid penis lying to one side, heavier than she would have expected. He moved his hair across his brow, gently, like a woman. He seemed unmoved by her appearance as if he had been expecting her.

Eloise stood in silence for a long moment. She heard the horn from a barge on the canal. Then she began to laugh. It was a deep laugh from down in her stomach, a panting almost, bringing her hand to her mouth, as she tried to hold the laughter back. Alexander was watching her, cautiously at first, then he was laughing too. He covered his legs with the quilt. Georges continued to towel himself then took his soap from a little dish, slathering his face with foam, looking over his shoulder in the mirror to the figure of Eloise looking over to Alexander Broady.

'Oh, I have been a fool,' Eloise said, tears in her eyes. Her laughter cut through with the occasional rootless sob. Georges drew the razor down his throat leaving raw pink oblongs. She felt like someone who had lost a fortune in the space of an afternoon and yet been lightened infinitely by it. She felt free. Yes, for the first time in her adult life she felt free.

*

The telephone in the hallway rang: the bells pinned to the lacquered box sounding, for a moment, like a frenzied exchange between two cyclists. Charles heaved himself from the chair in the drawing room where he had been dozing. His final meeting had run on longer than expected; there was a dispute with Ainscough's, regarding an outlet they claimed was depositing wastewater onto their property. He had given McDonald instructions not to budge despite their threats of legal action. 'He can threaten us all he likes. I was down there every day, and I can assure you there is no way on God's earth that water is coming from our pipes.'

'That's the spirit,' Charles had said, feeling as ever the indispensability of McDonald. He had sent a note to Cecil Ruislip informing him of their position, asking him to draft a letter to Ainscough. It had been seven before he left the office.

The telephone was still ringing, persistently, getting louder it seemed, if that were possible. It would be McDonald, he had been warning Charles for the past month that he needed to replace one of the vats, no doubt one had chosen this evening to catch light. Or he was calling to tell him about some new suppliers of japan wax he had found or a piano machine that was no longer cutting to size. The endless, incessant detail of it all. He often wondered how McDonald marshalled his informants across the various premises, those discrete streams of information. He had a genius for it. He would try and judge from McDonald's tone what was urgent and what was advisory. Though it always meant one thing – increased cost, week on week, month on month. As he approached the telephone, Charles speculated as to how much the conversation might cost him.

'Hello.'

'Mr Wright, this is Cecil Ruislip.'

'Yes, hello.'

'I'm calling regarding your sister, Miss Tabitha Wright.'

'What?'

*

Charles hurried down the steps, the stairwell curling sharply, his heels ringing on the stone. There were barred windows cut into each turn in the stairs, letting in a feeble yellow light from elsewhere in the building. A strong smell of urine and pumice. He walked briskly past a line of empty cells. In the final cell Tabitha sat alone.

'Charles, you must find out what happened to Eileen,' she called out.

'Are you here for her?' a constable asked, setting down the receiver on the telephone on the wall opposite her cell. He was squat man with a toothbrush moustache; the loose skin below his jaw was pockmarked.

'Husband, are you? You'll have to sign these.'

There was a ledger on the desk; the constable took a seat and removed his helmet. There was a line across his forehead where it had been pressing.

'Hasn't stopped rabbiting since we got her in. Last hour she's only had me to listen to her. Not stopped, have you, madam?' He shoved his tongue into his bottom lip; it became swollen like toad's neck. 'Be lucky to avoid the courts, won't you?'

'Can we hurry this along, please?'

The constable squinted at Charles. It was a look that seemed to contain both physical menace and legal threat.

'I trust you have the necessary documentation?'

Charles offered him the chits, signed and stamped upstairs where Cecil Ruislip was waiting, along with the cab driver Charles had insisted park and accompany them into the police station. There had been a delay as they attempted to locate Tabitha, the duty sergeant having no record of her arrest, dispatching an officer to find her who returned and explained she was being held in one of the basement cells.

The constable took the chits from Charles and examined them carefully, slapping them down like something poor quality and counterfeit he had recently confiscated.

*

Eloise made her way along the drive. The wet brick looked dazzling in the moonlight. She had yet to think of a plausible story to tell Charles about the lateness of her return or the whereabouts of his prized motor car. The Imperial was safe at least; Georges and Alexander had helped push it to a disused stable block at a dairy near Georges' lodgings. Alexander had promised to look in on it the next day. Nothing had been said about the scene into which Eloise had walked. Alexander had eventually risen and dressed, heaving his trousers up to his naked waist, looping the braces over his bare torso, retrieving his shirt from the floor. Georges had come in after shaving and offered her a small glass of astringent red wine. The three sat around the table and talked, as if her presence were the most ordinary thing in the world.

Eloise was sober now, or so she thought, but still she admired the glittering night hung around the leaves. She could hear an owl somewhere. Inside she clumsily removed her boots and stood for a moment at the entrance to the drawing room, peering at the gloom. There was a lit candle on the hearth.

'Tabitha? What are you doing up? Where's Charles?'

'He went to bed.'

She shifted on the sofa with a sharp intake of breath through her teeth.

'Tabitha, what's wrong? What's happened?'

She began to tell Eloise about the events at the Town Hall, her evening in the cells.

'I suppose you think I'm rather an idiot, don't you?'

'Will anything come of it?'

'Of what?'

'Of tonight, I mean, will you have to go to court?'

'Cecil Ruislip seemed to think not. We are to return to the police station tomorrow, I'm to present myself at one o'clock.'

'How did Charles take it?'

'Not entirely well.'

'No, I suspect he wouldn't.'

'He barely spoke a word to me on the way home.'

'I tell you what, shall we have some tea?'

Eloise returned a few minutes later carrying a tray on which was balanced a pair of mugs, a gravy boat and a sieve for removing soil from garden vegetables.

'I can never find anything without Cook,' she said, looking slightly ashamed.

The loose tea floated to the top of the gravy boat, the sisters carefully poured the contents over the sieve and into the mugs.

'And what on earth happened to you?' asked Tabitha.

'Oh, long story. I've made a decision.'

'Go on.'

'I'm leaving England.'

'When?'

'This summer.'

'With Monsieur Verstraeten?'

'Oh no.'

'How advanced are these plans?'

'Oh, fairly,' Eloise said.

'And have you spoken to Charles about this? Surely you won't leave without his blessing? You'll cause a scandal.'

'Well, yes, you've done me a favour in that respect.'

The clock on the mantelpiece chimed one. The pair sat quietly together. An owl called from somewhere high up in the garden. There was the cold smell of old cigar smoke.

'Do you remember, Tab, when Mama first took us to the house on Windermere?'

'When it was still owned by her uncle?'

'We must have been six or seven. I remember her telling us that one day this would be in ours, that it was our duty to look after it,'

'I remember.'

'I resented duty. My duty is whatever I decide. I can't stomach the idea that it's someone else's place to decide it for me.'

'You don't have to worry about the house, Charles has it all in hand.'

'If anything is to be in anyone's hands I'd like those hands to be mine.'

Eloise held up her hands as if she had newly discovered them.

'I'm sure tomorrow Mr Ruislip will take you to the police station, Charles will speak to some high-ups, and pfffff all will be well.'

'Don't be ridiculous.'

'Throw yourself from any height, fire yourself from any cannon, there will be a net to catch you.'

'I take it you wish to live a life divested of any of the comforts of your station?'

'Tabitha, you sound like Mr Ruislip.'

She paused then clutched a fist to her breast as if she had just driven a dagger into her own heart.

'I want the tightrope and the sheer drop. The fall that might kill me.'

'You are so dramatic.'

Eloise cupped her hand to her ear.

'Can you hear it, Tabitha, the world calling out to us? Come with me.'

'Where?'

'Paris or Copenhagen or Ankara, wherever I go.'

'What about poor Charles, who would look after him?'

'His wife, for one.'

'And Claude?'

Eloise curled her legs up on the sofa. She laid her head on her sister's lap. Tabitha began to run her hand over her hair.

'I shall miss you.'

'I expect you shall,' said Eloise, who yawned and closed her eyes.

1913

July

'And that is why –' he let the ascending voices fade, looking out at the smoke from the banqueting tables, as if he were viewing the city and its outlying districts from a hot-air balloon – 'we say: no. On this we shall not budge. The government may bury their heads if they wish –' he caught himself speeding up, becoming hectoring – 'but we shall not. Tariff reform, gentlemen, is the order of the day and by God it is the only order.'

Applause. Men's features warped by candlelight. At some unseen signal, a dozen waiters were gliding between the tables with platters of veined cheese and dark grapes. From where Charles stood it seemed balletic, dancers funnelling onto a stage. He had the audience now, he could feel it. The magnetism of their collective attention. It had been piecemeal at first, conversations burbling on as he began his speech, but now he had them, each and every one.

'Pairs, gentlemen; I am told good things come in them.' He leaned forward on the lectern. 'A lion and a lamb. A sword and a stone. A tariff and a freeze.' He straightened himself to his full height. 'A moderate tariff on foreign manufactured goods and a long overdue freeze on duties.'

Someone banged their table, others followed. Charles took his chance to improvise.

'This government has lurched from calamity to calamity, have they not?'

Voices rose in agreement.

'We have seen them, we have seen them for what they are; Mr Lloyd George pilloried by one of our own last week, outed as a mere controversialist. Well, here is an uncontroversial statement for you, gentlemen: what our country needs now is not more Lloyd George but more George Lloyd.'

He gestured with a stern stabbing motion to the Right Honourable Member for Staffordshire West seated at the central table, his dark moustache trimmed above the lip, the small lithe man who had once coxed the Cambridge crew. There was raucous laughter and cries of 'Hear, hear!' He had more to say, on Ulster, on Land Taxes, but there were more speeches to come, better to be remembered for wit and brevity than for taking up too much time after supper. Glazebrook had only invited him to speak when a more senior representative of the textile industry had fallen from his horse and broken his back out riding to hounds.

'Thank you.' He slid his notes into his dinner jacket, and made his way down from the stage. Aitken was there, looking as if he had overindulged, and Lancelot Sanderson; both men nodded at Charles. Then Sanderson rose, with a brandy glass and a long cigar in one hand, slapping Charles on the shoulder as one might strike the flank of a winning horse entering a paddock.

'Fine fellow,' Charles heard Sanderson say to Aitken who murmured something non-committal.

After the speeches had finished the guests began to drift from the banqueting hall. A lone voice embarked on a verse of 'Rule Britannia' but it failed to take and petered out. Glazebrook and Sanderson, both very red with drink, and a third man who looked quite sober, were standing in the Winter Garden. They were discussing going on to a card room and asked Charles if he would join them.

'My driver is here and I am an appalling gambler. I lose every time.'

'Well, lunch then, here, tomorrow,' said Sanderson.

'I should be delighted.'

'Now, gentlemen,' said the third man impatiently to Glazebrook and Sanderson, 'shall we see if we can't find ourselves some brass?' He smiled, revealing large teeth like discoloured ivory.

Charles bid goodnight to the doorman at the entrance to the hotel. He scanned the street for his driver. Four cars down in the waiting row he saw headlights brighten then dim. He made his way to the landaulet, as Benzie, in his grey suit and cap, opened the door. There was someone inside and for a moment Charles thought he had made a mistake.

'I hope you don't mind me coming. We've had a letter.'

Tabitha held it up like a winning ticket from a tombola. She was wearing a pair of slippers and a dressing gown. Her hair was tied with what looked like a piece of garden twine. Charles took a seat beside her. A gentleman appeared at the window.

'One moment,' Charles said, brusquely, to his sister. She had been hounding him about Farthing Bundles, which involved concerned citizens sending impoverished children dolls made from old newspaper and kindling. It seemed ludicrous. He slid down his window.

'Glad I caught you,' the man said; he was wearing a tightly fitting army parade jacket, and the elasticity had gone from his undereyes. 'Damn good speech, damn good.' He clutched at the window then leaned heavily through to shake Charles's hand, rocking the landaulet towards him.

'Thank you,' Charles said, tucking his gloves into his top hat, offering his hand to the man.

'From the heart,' the man said, gripping Charles's hand. 'Heart,' he repeated, tapping his fist below a row of jangling medals. 'You have my vote.'

'That's very good of you.'

The man looked at Tabitha with a wince of incomprehension. He seemed on the verge of comment but a group of men passed and he turned away, calling for them to stop.

'That's the Lord Lieutenant of Cheshire.'

'He looks like he's been enjoying the evening.'

'Very shrewd man.'

'Perhaps he would like to contribute to the Mission? Do you have an address at which I might write to him?'

'Thank you, Benzie, home please,' said Charles, ignoring his sister.

Benzie released the brake. There was a swift surge of power as the automobile moved off, past the Lord Lieutenant who was staggering towards the waiting group.

'Charles, it's from Eloise in America.'

He turned to face his sister.

'The letter. Dolly mentioned it this evening – it's been sitting on your desk all day. I ran upstairs at once to retrieve it. I hope you don't think it rude of me?'

Charles raised his brow.

'She has included a cutting from the *Chicago Tribune* in which she is mentioned by name. Shall I read it?'

'Do I have a choice?' Charles said, looking over notes he had made from the evening on the back of his menu.

'"Amongst the extraordinary detritus of the Armory Show which arrived this week in Chicago, Miss Eloise Wright's work stands out as at least marginally connected to the august traditions of European painting."' Tabitha pressed the cutting to her chest. 'She says she's terribly disappointed she didn't cause more of a stir and that a painting of hers has sold to someone from the Carnegie Steel Company.'

'I'm glad her career is proving lucrative. That's what, let me see now, income of – how much did the picture sell for?'

'One hundred and fifty-five dollars.'

'Which gives us I believe thirty-one pounds or there-abouts at the current rate of exchange, set against expenditure –' he took a silver pencil from his breast pocket, drawing a box below his notes on the back of the menu – 'of let's say twenty pounds a month for the years she was in Paris, a further twenty-five this past spell in New York, not to mention supplementary expenses of thirty or so pounds per annum, giving a total of one thousand seven hundred and ten pounds expenditure with an income of one hundred and fifty dollars –'

'Fifty-five –'

'I'm sorry, you're quite right, one hundred and fifty-five dollars or thirty-one pounds sterling thereabouts –' Charles held the number up to Tabitha for her to confirm his arithmetic. 'Money soundly invested.'

'Charles, can't you simply be content for her?' But his attention had already returned to the notes on the back of his menu.

All along Oxford Street the theatres and music halls were turning out. Couples with their arms around each other or running to catch the omnibus. A man was playing an accordion on the corner, a small crowd gathered around him.

'It seems I have enough votes for the nomination,' Charles said, almost to himself. He unbuttoned his jacket, the swell of his stomach relaxed outwards. 'What is that in your hair?'

Tabitha touched her hair.

'I was in a rush to catch Benzie when I heard the car.'

'Bizarre.'

It was Tabitha's turn to ignore Charles.

'She says she'll be back in ten days' time.'

'A few more,' he continued, 'and my candidacy will be all but assured. I'm sorry, what did you say?'

'The RMS *Carmania* to Liverpool. Eloise.'

'I hope she doesn't intend to do anything to embarrass me.'

'Charles, really.'

'This is not some hobby, Tabitha.'

He redid his jacket, adjusted his tie as if readying himself to take the stage again.

'Benzie, stop here,' he said, tapping him on the shoulder.

He swung the door and jumped from the landaulet, into a puddle at the pavement's edge. He returned a few moments later with two copies of the *Manchester Courier*.

'Want to see if my speech made the late edition.'

Tabitha looked down at his shoes. They were soaking wet.

'Well, don't just stare, make yourself useful.'

He passed her a copy of the newspaper.

'Here,' Tabitha said eventually, '"Textile Heir Sparkles at Party Dinner".'

'See, our sister isn't the only one making the news.'

Charles carefully tore the article out and placed it in his breast pocket along with the menu, then wiped his shoes with what remained of the newspaper.

*

Tabitha looked across the breakfast table; the marmalade jar – a dazzle of light in its cut-glass sides, the triangles of toast in their pewter rack. Charles had yet to rise, she had heard him thumping around his study after they returned from the hotel last night, and Hettie always took breakfast alone in her room. Tabitha had been enjoying the quiet, the cut flowers, the pristine cloth. As it was Saturday she wasn't due at the Mission until four; until then the morning stretched out. A figure in white seemed to glide past the doorway.

'Good morning, Aunt Tabitha.'

'Claude, look at you,' she said, putting down her book.

He was wearing a pair of flannel trousers with a sharp crease, a white shirt and a cable-knitted cardigan.

'Are those new whites?'

'Mama bought them for me. I think I look rather smart. Smart but deadly.'

He bent with his tennis racket in two hands, moving his weight from foot to foot.

'Observe also one pair of buckskin rubber-soled tennis oxfords.'

He had played twice a week for the past month; his face was lightly tanned, deepening to a soft clay redness around the back of his neck and his ears.

'What time is your match?'

'Twelve. There's a doubles tournament but I need to mend this first.'

He turned his racket towards Tabitha. Three of the strings had snapped and ran in frayed zigzags down the face.

'Demon, Pastime, Service and Cannes,' he said, placing the racket on the table, 'they're the big four. This is a Demon – an Ordinary, mind you, not a Special.'

'Do you plan to mend it yourself?'

'There's a man at the club, Walton, who will restring it for a shilling – ninepence if you take the strings out first.'

He unscrewed the frame and began trying to tease out one of the snapped strings.

'Are you done with that?' he said, nodding at the rack of toast.

Claude pulled a slice from the rack, clumsily buttered it, then set a blob of marmalade at its centre which he squashed down with the back of a spoon.

'Your father has a fairly large staff, they will prepare most breakfasts.'

'But someone else's always tastes so much better,' he said, wedging the toast in his mouth, as he tried again to work the broken string loose.

'The small sins of the saintly … '

'Who's to say I'm saintly?' he replied with a smirk.

He placed his toast on the table, a buttery mark spreading on the cloth. He splayed then clenched his fingers.

'So what's that then?' he asked as he dragged a cup and saucer across the table towards him.

'Nothing that would interest you.'

'Aunt Tab, you'd be surprised, I've a *Wisden's* upstairs, cover's practically falling off it, best shilling I ever spent.'

'This,' she said, raising her book, 'is *A Critical and Exegetical Commentary on the Book of Isaiah* by George Buchanan Gray.'

'Cease to do evil, learn to do well; seek out the right.' Claude listed the injunctions as if they had radically curtailed his own life so far.

'Very good.'

'Rather early in the day for all that, isn't it?' he said. 'I worry you may have been spending too long at the Mission – you'll be bound for Calabar next.'

'Claude Wright, you are an exceedingly rude young man,' Tabitha said, pouring tea in a loose brown ribbon from the slender spout, with a smile she could not quite suppress.

The sound of the door knocker echoed through the house sudden as gunfire. Tabitha glanced at Claude. He made his way along the hall buttoning his cardigan. When he unbolted the door he was greeted by the backs of two heads. One of them turned.

'Claude! My God! Look at you!'

Eloise embraced her nephew. Her hair was cut into a short bob. He stood stiffly, arms by his sides.

'Look at you! A grown man.' She squeezed his shoulder as if to confirm he was there, then held his arm up and had him spin for her like a ballerina in a music box.

Tabitha stood a few paces behind Claude.

'But we weren't expecting you for another ten days.'

'I know, we took an earlier boat.'

'What have you done to your hair?'

'Do you think it rather outré?' Eloise turned to her sister, jutting a hip, dropping her chin. 'You should have seen me when I first had it all done, I looked like Claude here. The grocer called me *petit bonhomme*. Isn't that right, Bessie?'

Beside Eloise stood a solid-looking woman in a bat-winged cardigan, fastened with an amber brooch. She had cheeks that sagged below her jaw, a round chin, dark, slightly hooded eyes. Her hair was shot through with grey, pinned in a tight, inexpert crown.

'Claude, allow me to introduce my great friend, patron and travelling companion, Miss Bessie Montana.'

'Handsome boy,' Bessie said, gripping Claude's hand, 'reminds me of Gaston Modot,' then turning to Tabitha, 'Modot is a very fine young actor making something of a name for himself in Montmartre,' then to Eloise, 'you met him at the dinner I gave for Polaire, Maurice Tourner brought him along,' then back to Tabitha, 'they'd made a moving picture about some halfwit who buys a Rembrandt for thirty-five francs in a cafe on Rue Lepic,' before finally addressing Claude in a semi-confidential tone, 'there's very little one can get for thirty-five francs on Rue Lepic these days,' and stepping past him, without invitation, into the house.

*

The family were assembled in the drawing room. Claude had gone to help retrieve their trunks from the waiting motor taxi. Dolly brought through the tray, set bone china on a low table.

'And tell me,' Charles said, 'Montana, is that a common name?'

'The story has it my grandfather saw it on a map after he arrived to trap fur with the Blackfoot Confederacy. I've come to doubt that as the Montana Territory only came into being by Act of Congress in '64. Before going west he'd worked as a wolver, slaying the cattle-killing grey by the thousand.'

She gave a low laugh and then turned in her seat towards the door.

'And who is this?' she asked as if a slow child or shy dog had come into the room.

'My God, Hettie, hello,' Eloise said, getting to her feet. Hettie's hair was white; it came down to below her shoulders.

'Mama,' said Claude, rising to greet her, kissing her softly on both cheeks. 'Will you join us?' He gestured to the table. His mother remained standing.

'I hope you are very comfortable during your stay, Miss Montana.' She spoke in a tiny dry voice. 'We are very pleased to have you here. And in the interest you have taken in Eloise. We went to America once, didn't we, Charles?'

'Was this after Cambridge?' Bessie asked.

'I gave all that up, Natural Sciences not much use once I made up my mind to go into business,' Charles said, with a bullishness over which he didn't quite have full possession.

'So you didn't take your degree?' asked Claude.

'Deferred. I believe university statutes say I could go back for it if I wished.'

'You've retained an interest in botany,' said Hettie, as if there were something vaguely improper about it.

'I chair the board for the Cactus House at Alexandra Park –' he was on more certain ground now – 'knocks Kew into a cocked hat. The cacti were left to the Corporation by a man named Darrah. Made his money in lead. No expense spared assembling it; West Indies, Mexico, Peru.'

'I find them grotesque,' said Hettie.

'Some of them are quite different from anything else in the vegetable kingdom, we've three and a half thousand specimens looked after by a very capable man named Cobbald.'

'Do they flower?' asked Eloise, stirring a cube of sugar into her tea.

'The floral recommendations are fairly trivial,' said Charles.

'In Peru they use the spikes for fish hooks,' said Tabitha.

'Quite right,' said Charles. 'I'm sure you know, Miss Montana, in America a man might survive for months on cacti alone – slice an *Echinocactus* and you've water, while the fruit of the *Opuntia* will serve as food.'

There was a lull in the conversation. Tabitha took it upon herself to restart it.

'Please, do tell us more about your recent trip.'

'What raised eyebrows in New York was positively libellous out on the Great Plains,' said Bessie.

'Was that very distressing?' Tabitha asked.

'Not at all,' said Bessie. 'We were delighted.'

'You'll have heard about our own recent drama at the gallery,' Charles said.

'Charles is a member of the board there too,' Tabitha explained.

'The attendant heard the smashing glass. Watts, Burne-Jones, Rossetti, a big Millais. I was at the assizes with Peacock, the chief constable. This Forrester woman gave some rambling cant, claiming she was a patriot. Well, I've the bills for the repair work upstairs, tell me what is patriotic about that.'

'Good for them,' said Bessie, drawing a brief look of incomprehension from Charles.

'And what are your first impressions of the city, Miss Montana?' asked Tabitha.

'I had pictured a miasma of smoke and fog. But it seems Eloise's stories have been untrue – fine rain and green trees are all I have encountered.'

'Plenty of smoke a few miles in. I'm sure Claude would be happy to show you. We have one of the oldest calico printing operations in the country.'

'I should like that.'

'Well, see to it Miss Montana gets to view all the places of interest,' said Charles, 'Perhaps McDonald can accompany you.'

'Very well,' said Claude obediently as he gently helped his mother through the door and towards the stairs, his hand not quite touching her back.

'Striking woman,' Bessie said to Eloise. 'That hair must take a God-awful amount of brushing. I'm glad I'm not her lady's maid.'

*

The general office sat between the boiler house and the coal yard. A drab-looking cube of chestnut brick. Stems of buddleia, lilac at their tips, grew from cracks in the masonry. The building seemed squat among the high banks of lighted windows in the Wright & Co. complex. Eloise remembered visiting in childhood, her mother's injunction she must not interrupt her father as he walked ahead, the cool, clean smell of the finished cloth. Eloise paused to adjust the belt on her suit, honeycomb hexagons on the wide turquoise collar. The motor taxi had driven her into the centre of the mill, the gatekeeper opening the swing barrier to the lane usually reserved for wagons carrying finished cloth. It was raining as she dashed across the cobbles, the motor taxi waiting as instructed, the driver looking out over his spare wheel, as Eloise made her way inside having promised she would be back soon.

Claude stood from behind his desk. He wore his shirt-sleeves rolled to above his elbows, a narrow necktie in a four-hand knot. There was a softness to him, an openness to his face, which had grown handsome albeit in a boyish way. The tin-ceilinged office was separated by a thin wall from the samples room beyond. The desk beside Claude's belonged to McDonald. There was a set of technical drawings spread across it. McDonald was going through registration cards from the machine shop.

'I thought I'd take you to lunch,' said Eloise.

'You should have called ahead,' Claude said, gesturing to the compact wooden box fixed to the wall behind McDonald's desk.

'Yes, but then I should have had to speak with Mr McDonald.'

'I mustn't be too long, they struggle without me,' said Claude, then louder, 'don't you?'

McDonald shook his head and began writing something very precisely in a ledger.

'Back by one please, Mr Wright,' he said without looking up.

'Nonsense, darling, we shall be as long as we like,' Eloise whispered, and once they were beyond the door added, 'No privileges for you, I see.'

'None whatsoever,' Claude said, retrieving his jacket from the coat rack. 'Treated the same as anyone, point of honour.'

'Well, it won't last forever.'

'Oh, I don't mind one bit.'

Eloise drew the corner off a roll of cloth, holding it across her face like a figure from *Arabian Nights*.

'Don't think McDonald would be too pleased to see his samples in disarray.'

She pushed the reel over; it sent several more clattering down. Behind the glass of the door they saw McDonald rise from his desk.

'Better scarper,' Eloise said, taking Claude by the wrist, running down the stairs and across the cobbles to the waiting taxi whose driver seemed relieved his exotic-looking fare had finally returned.

Twenty minutes later they were standing by a rack of ties on the third floor of Pauldens.

'Tell me, Claude, have you a sweetheart?'

Eloise held a lavender silk bow to Claude's throat, then another, midnight blue with tiny white polka dots, in its place.

'I'm afraid not,' Claude said, keeping his head still as he acted as mannequin.

'Strapping lad like you, there must be someone, at the Tennis Club perhaps?'

'Oh no, I'm far too busy for any of that,' he said with a sort of smirk.

'I don't believe you.'

'So what have you been doing?' Claude asked.

'Oh, this and that.'

'I always enjoyed the cards you sent. I have them all.'

'What a good nephew you are. Tell me – do you enjoy your work?'

'Yes, though I'm still learning. McDonald knows so much about the business, right back to my grandfather's day. He's some marvellous stories about his time in the Transvaal. He and some pals took a Long Tom at Ladysmith. Crept inside in the dead of night, wrecked its muzzle with a charge of gun cotton. Made off with the breech block as a trophy. Told me he thought I was officer material.'

After buying Claude two shirts and a silk bow tie, they made their way, on Claude's recommendation, to the Albion Hotel on the corner of Oldham Street and Piccadilly; a row of new canvas awnings looked out onto the interchange of tramlines. A waiter, whom Claude seemed to know, led them through the Coffee Room into the vaulted ceiling of the restaurant, forty uniform tables with white cloths.

'I shall have a glass of the Rüdesheimer.'

'Nothing for me, thank you,' said Claude.

'My nephew here shall have the same.'

'Do you think Miss Montana will be staying long?'

'I shouldn't think so,' said Eloise, 'I imagine she just wanted to take the measure of your father.'

'My father?'

'She takes an interest in the home lives of all the artists she supports.'

'I see,' said Claude tactfully.

'How's your mother?' Eloise asked. 'I've barely seen her.'

'Oh, you know Mother. She has her ways, at the moment it's Christian Science. Heal the sick, raise the dead, cast out demons,' Claude said with a good-hearted yet not quite believing laugh. 'Last year it was the Fur, Fin and Feather Folk or whatever they're calling themselves these days. Over Easter she had Dolly throw out all manner of hats, boas, dresses. A good day to be an egret.'

Eloise laughed.

'Though she entered one of her slumps afterwards.'

'I see.'

'She's very kind to me, you know, she just gets so tired.'

'Is there nothing that can be done?'

'Aunt Tabitha suggested a nature cure in Meadstead.'

'A nature cure?'

'Vapour baths, air huts, a rigorously enforced diet. Father dismissed the idea. Now Aunt Tabitha has to hide her copies of the *New Age* whenever it arrives. Seditionist bunkum he calls it.'

The food was wheeled to the table. A waiter in a white shift carved, with a long pearl-handled knife, pale slices of pork shoulder.

'You know you looked like your father just then.'

'Don't tell him, he'll be delighted,' said Claude, tucking into his food.

'How did you know that boy on the way in?'

He seemed to colour a little.

'Oh, Father brought me here for a Rotarians lunch earlier in the year, he was awfully keen to make a good impression. This will amuse you, as we were leaving we inadvertently walked in on an auction.'

Eloise was on the verge of asking another question about the boy but stopped herself.

'Something exciting, I hope?' she said 'Diamonds? Motor cars?'

'The pier at Rhyl, believe it or not,' Claude laughed, 'along with some buildings and a parcel of land on the foreshore.'

'Did you bid?'

'I encouraged Father to. Came with its own Bijou Theatre and Refreshment Room.'

'Can't imagine he was tempted.'

'Not sure how it would sit with the Rotarians. Out of good manners he made us wait until the auction had finished before we left.'

'Did it make its reserve?'

'Not a single bidder. Now, Aunt Eloise, here's a question for you, what was the name of that Frenchman you brought to the house in Windermere, when I was a boy?' Claude asked, sawing into his pork.

'Belgian, Monsieur Verstraeten, Georges Verstraeten.'

'That's it, yes,' Claude said, brightening as he recalled the visit. 'I was thinking of him only the other day.' He stabbed a piece of pork, which he then dabbed in his apple sauce. 'Do you ever hear of him?' He took a sip from his wine. When no answer came he looked up from his lunch.

'A friend wrote to me last year telling me Mr Verstraeten had been killed in an automobile accident.'

'I am so sorry.'

'Yes, so was I.' Eloise's voice seemed to dry up. There were tears in her eyes. She wiped them away with the tip of her finger. 'Look at me. Here, pass me that napkin.'

Claude handed the napkin to her. She attempted to eat some of her own lunch, then pushed the plate to one side and took a sip from her wine.

'How old are you, Claude?'

'I'm twenty-three.'

'Did the varsity never appeal?'

'I attended for a term. I found it all rather, well, dull. Father suggested I come and work for him. I think it was supposed to shock me back there. Truth is, I don't much mind the work. That was almost four years ago.'

'And will you stay?'

'Father thinks I should consider the Army.'

'Oh, Claude, the Army?'

'Believes a commission might help me get along.'

He had eaten almost everything on his plate save half a new potato which he now used to swab up the remaining apple sauce.

'Father seems to have his mind set on it, if not the regulars then the Yeomanry.'

He seemed to accept his father's view without reflection.

'Now, as I am your aunt you must tell the truth. If none of this existed, no rolls of cloth, no Rotarians, what would you most like to spend your time doing?'

'Aside from running the Bijou Theatre on the pier at Rhyl?'

'Aside from that.'

'Well,' Claude said, setting down his knife and fork and reclining, his hands with their clean nails, folded neatly across his stomach, 'I should like to breed ponies.'

'Ponies?'

'Shetlands, Father's friend has some. They're the most fascinating creatures, much nastier than people imagine.'

'Claude, I can't tell if you're joking.'

'Oh no, I'm quite serious.'

*

What sounded at first like a fracas or a quarrel revealed itself on approaching to be raucous laughter. Gathered at the far end of the kitchen were Cook, Dolly and Dolly's daughter Esme, a nervous girl with red hair, very pale skin. As Charles drew near, the group fell into a hush. Miss Montana turned to see what had caused the change in her previously attentive audience.

'I was just telling these girls about the buffalo.' She formed two primitive horns with her thumbs and forefingers. Dolly and her daughter suppressed more giggling. 'My father had one mounted on my nursery wall – imagine that, girls, a buffalo looking down on you in the cradle.'

Charles looked coldly at the servants.

'I expect Mr Wright has all manner of work for you to be getting along with.'

The group dissolved. Before Charles could demur, Bessie linked his arm and led him to the drawing room. She gestured to an armchair between the unlit fire and a mahogany drinks cabinet, as if she were hosting him.

'Do you know Esme wishes to be a seamstress?'

She pulled the plug from a glass decanter, then poured a measure of Scotch into a crystal tumbler.

'I did not.'

'And that your cook is sixty-four next April?'

'Again, you have the advantage.'

'I can't abide servants,' Bessie Montana said, settling herself in the chair opposite Charles. 'They clutter places up, or else take offence at the smallest things. But those are fine girls.'

Charles smiled perfunctorily.

'So I understand you have spent the past year with my sister?'

'I predict one hell of a future for her.'

He plucked a piece of dust from his lapel, smoothed it with his fingertips.

'And may I ask what your plans are?'

'We've a berth booked on the steamboat from Bordeaux to Galveston, Texas, December first, and from there it's the railroad to Arizona. I've a ranch house looked after by Pueblo Indians. But we shall see out the summer here in England.'

'You intend to travel to Arizona with Eloise?'

'I hope your sister will produce her first mature work there. We've grasslands, meadows, the Santa Rita Mountains in the distance. A whole herd of javelina – skunk pigs we call them. The Benson–Nogales Railroad ships five thousand head of cattle daily to the East. My father bought the place the year before he died. Adobe houses dotted all across it. I've promised your sister the run of one. We've no servants, unless you count the Indians who fairly well do as they please. We do our own washing, floor-scrubbing; the place breeds practical people.'

'Miss Montana, in Paris I am able to make regular visits to my sister. I have acquaintances in the city that she can turn to should she need assistance. I am sure you understand having an unmarried sister living alone is Paris is one thing, but to have her travelling to corners of the New World with –'

'This old hag?' Bessie gave an immense, bellowing laugh.

'I think it's liable to attract the very worst kind of attention.'

Hettie came into the room and looked at the pair uncomprehendingly, as if she had discovered two tramps at rest.

'Am I disturbing you?' she asked.

'Not at all,' said Bessie, raising her glass.

'Miss Montana intends to take my sister to Arizona.'

'Is it not rather dangerous?' asked Hettie.

'Only if you are a rebel constitutionalist. Besides, Eloise enjoys a little danger.'

Bessie rose and helped herself to more whisky.

'Mr Wright, there is something you must understand: Lillie Bliss has never beaten me to anything and I've been buying work from under the nose of Louisine Havemeyer for aeons. Not long ago I travelled to the Villa Curonia to visit Mabel Dodge.' She turned to Hettie and lowered her voice. 'She's had a difficult spell, fell for her chauffeur, tried to take her own life. Twice. Second time with laudanum, the first eating figs with shards of glass. But, you see, unlike those girls I never married a single cent that I own. It makes all the difference.' She turned to Charles and raised her glass. 'Disregard my sex – I assure you it is the only way you will tolerate me in your home.'

'I shall try my level best,' said Charles with more tartness than intended.

*

A weak sun was inching around the pines behind the grass courts. The net sagged, wire showing through the worn cloth. There were parched ovals by the service lines; the courts beside them were empty. Tabitha removed the frame from the head of her racket. Her sister fired a ball over the net; it struck her skirt with a thud.

'My serve,' said Eloise as she strutted along the service line.

'A few rallies first perhaps.'

'Is Charles really going to run for Parliament?'

'Hopes to, there's a seat in Cheshire.'

'I always thought he was a Liberal.'

'So did he, but he had a terrible falling-out with a man called Arthur Haworth, now Sir Arthur. I don't know if you saw in the papers?'

Eloise shook her head.

'All got rather nasty when he blocked Charles's appointment to the board of the Exchange. Charles claimed it was a fix-up – something to do with Dilworths, where Sir Arthur is a partner, wanting to move into one of our markets.'

'Gosh,' said Eloise.

'Also, and I've no idea why, but our brother seems to have become absolutely fixated on tariff reform.'

Tabitha reached for a return from Eloise which went bobbling off the end of her racket. She walked over to the court's edge where the ball had come to rest among a patch of dandelions.

'I must admit he has a gift for public speaking. Campaigned for Glazebrook in the by-election after Sir Arthur was appointed Lord Commissioner to the Treasury.'

Tabitha served, receiving a gentle return which just managed to make it over the net, then bounced softly on the grass. She picked the ball up and stepped back to the service line.

'The irony is the only reason Sir Arthur won in 1910 was because Glazebrook turned up late to the Town Hall, after the nominations had closed, his agent's fault apparently. Well, no such bad luck in the by-election. Not with Charles campaigning for him. Ever since, Glazebrook and Charles have been thick as thieves. He won by only a few hundred votes and a good deal of those I put down to Charles.'

'What's this Glazebrook chap like then?'

'Rather odd.' Tabitha whacked the ball back to emphasise her point. 'Family sell oil, Farrier and Glazebrook's. Charles is often there at weekends. He is likely to stand should there be another by-election any time soon and if not there's a feeling he'll be put forward as a candidate whenever the next election is called, which I suppose must be sometime in 1916.'

'That seems a long way off.'

Tabitha had begun to perspire and wiped her face with a handkerchief.

'Shall we take a break?'

The pair sat on a bench at the side of the court, fanning themselves. A family with two boys in sailor suits and a Pomeranian walked past.

'Tell me the shape of your days,' Tabitha asked. 'You give away so little in your letters.'

'I've a studio I share with a woman named Arabella Gladstone. I must have told you about her? It's a smallish room, high ceiling, hard to heat. I paint until early afternoon then cycle over to the studio of Monsieur Vallier, who

I assist four afternoons a week. He's from a little town in the Rhône-Alpes though has lived in Paris for forty years, huge unwashed moustache full of tobacco and marble dust. His pieces sell for thousands. He's fairly dour but he is the most exquisite craftsman and he always pays me on time and each season he throws a party for his collectors. Awfully good fun; ballerinas, opera singers, senators, the whole lot.'

'Amazing you ever get any work done.'

Eventually the sisters restarted the game.

'And how exactly does one come to meet someone like Miss Montana?'

'Oh, the way one does,' Eloise said, returning the ball. 'We were at the apartment of an English painter, Julian White. It was late so there were only a few of us; Julian was playing a mandolin he had bought at the flea market. All of a sudden there was this tremendous hammering on the door — we thought it was the gendarmerie. To all of our surprise, it was a man named Vollard, who has a gallery on Rue Laffitte, and he was with Bessie. Vollard and Bessie were fairly ripe with drink, and she was insisting on meeting the finest young painters in the city. Julian was, at that time at least, considered one of them. Bessie came upstairs and drank all that remained of our wine then invited Julian, Arabella and myself to lunch the next day at the Gare de Lyon. For some reason I suspect still haunts him, Julian took offence at something Bessie had said, so it was only myself and Arabella. We cycled down and as it happened

Bessie's driver was dropping her and Vollard at that exact moment. Seeing us with the bicycles just delighted Bessie. She must have only had an hour or so's sleep yet she was irrepressible. Vollard left for a train to Geneva, then Arabella went too. Bessie and I sat and talked, three hours or more. She's been everywhere, Guinea, Bali, told me she once took a samurai as a lover and had to flee Japan fearing the wrath of the shogunate.'

'And you believed her?'

'I had no reason not to. It was through her my work was selected for the Armory. She is formidable, isn't she?' Eloise sent the tennis ball with a soft pock over the net. 'My first great patron.'

There was another soft pock as Tabitha knocked the ball back to Eloise who stretched to return it but missed then stumbled.

'You are not, well, how should I put this ... well, what exactly is the nature of your relationship?'

Eloise stopped and picked up the ball. She walked towards the net.

'Tabitha, what have you been reading? You'll be asking if Miss Montana and I are amorously involved next. Do we nightly consort in dimly lit bordellos under the influence of hashish? Now come on, let's play for points.'

It was three games all before the sisters began to talk again.

'And how about you, Tabitha — any romantic entanglements?'

Tabitha frowned and moved forward again to receive Eloise's serve.

'Do you remember Mr Allardyce?'

'The insect man?'

'We corresponded briefly before he left for Patagonia. And you?'

'There was an eye doctor on the Rue du Delta who tried to convince me to go and live in an artists' colony he was setting up. The place was appalling, filthy, squalid, malodorous, terrible light. They all seem to think I'm far younger than I am.'

Tabitha played a drop shot which Eloise lurched forward to reach.

'I've always been able to live quite well on my allowance. You see these silly boys squandering it all in the creameries and at the model market on Montparnasse, then going without soap for a month. Things have changed since Bessie took an interest, my studio is much warmer, and there are fewer men attempting to save me, which I very much approve of. I've a growing circle of collectors. Before we left for America we dined at the house of Edmond Sagot. He bought a set of etchings from me, of jugglers. His brother Clovis was once a clown at the Medrano Circus. Bessie thinks she can get him to take a couple of my larger canvases.'

The game petered out, the sisters making less and less effort to return each other's shots. When Eloise sent the ball off into the pines both sisters returned to the bench with their rackets.

'Ellie, will you do something for me?'

'Anything.'

'Do you have plans this evening?'

*

'You'll need this.' Tabitha handed Eloise an oilskin. It was dark outside, rain hammering down after clinging to the gables of the nearby villas all afternoon.

'Could we not ask Benzie to run us to wherever it is we're going?'

Eloise was at the window of the drawing room, the raincape folded over her arm, holding back the curtain, addressing the watery image of her sister out on the drive.

'I don't think so,' said Tabitha, as she fastened then smoothed down her own cape. 'He'll be in bed by now I should imagine,' she added, a touch brusquely.

They set off on their bicycles, crunching down the gravel path, out onto the street lined with elms and elders, the neighbouring villas set behind dense hedgerows and coping stones grown mossy in the years since they were laid. Tabitha was ahead, streams of water sent up as the bicycles moved along the road. She stopped, turned and called to her sister, 'Shall we go via the park? I know a gate that may be open.'

Eloise, who had paused to adjust her cape, called back, 'Oh yes, let's, it's years since I saw it.'

They started pedalling again, spokes flashing where light struck the rainwater and steel.

As Tabitha had promised, a gate on the perimeter was open. They went in, lifting their bicycles over the step. Inside they set off towards the west edge of the park, freewheeling down a hill, past a boating lake where empty rowing boats bobbed beside lily pads. A massive glass building loomed in the darkness, its gable painted white. They continued towards it, rested their bicycles against the wall. Eloise inspected herself in the glass, pressing her face close up. The cacti were faintly visible in the moonlight falling through the glass ceiling with its scrolling metalwork.

'Is this the place Charles is involved with?'

'Yes, he sits on the board.'

'If I were a cactus come all the way from Mexico I think I would have given up the will to grow upon arrival.'

'There's one in there named for him. Recently flowering, smells of honeysuckle. From a place called Ixmiquilpan. Don't ask me how to spell it.'

'I see you've been keeping busy.'

'The only other place it's ever flowered is New York.'

Tabitha climbed up the flight of steps that led to a side door of the Cactus House. She tried the handle, rattling it.

'What are you doing, Tab?' Eloise called up.

Tabitha came down the stairs and placed her hands at various angles around some of the smaller windows. She took a notebook from her pocket and wrote something down.

'Well, must push on, come along, Ellie.'

She kicked the stand from her bicycle and set off, leaving her sister to catch up.

The line of people stretched around the building with its black downpipes and iron-edged paving stones. At the front of the queue a mongrel with a missing eye, a furred depression scooped from the side of its face, was trotting in circles around its owner's feet.

'What is this place?'

'It's the soup kitchen at the Mission,' said Tabitha. 'Don't worry, they won't bite.'

'Hello, Sammy,' Tabitha said. 'How are we today?'

'Still here, miss.'

His face had an angular quality to it. He wore a flat cap and a thick collarless shirt.

'How's Cissie?'

'Fine, hard at it.' He nodded towards the kitchen. Some of his bottom teeth were missing; he worked his tongue into the gaps between words.

'Samuel was an iron fitter at Duckworth's until they saw fit to let him go, but thankfully for us, since December he's been our hall keeper.'

'So how does it work?' Eloise asked, surveying the busy kitchen, the row of empty tables and the long queue outside.

'We toyed with the idea of giving out tickets, charging tuppence, thought it might be better for the balance sheet, what with gas, rates, rent, furniture repairs, hall keeper's wages, though we don't begrudge you those, Samuel,' Tabitha said. 'Believe it or not most of those who come here are in work, though we do get our share of idlers and vagrants. We rely on donations. I pestered Charles and finally managed to raise some money from the Exchange. Perhaps your Miss Montana would like to make a donation?' Tabitha asked, flashing Eloise a cool, firm smile.

'I'm sure she would.'

'Good,' said Tabitha, 'saves me writing to her. Our ambition is to raise enough so the Mission can run in perpetuity, from interest on capital. Our All Are Welcome policy puts some people off. They think us a seat of vice – they might not be wrong if they'd seen what Lily Callaghan was up to in the back room last Easter.'

'Oh, do tell.'

'Well, put it like this, I suggested she donate half to the Mission, along with extracting a promise she would not undertake such work for the next year.'

'Do you get to know many of them?'

'Some,' said Tabitha. 'It's more the running of the place I'm involved with, making sure the likes of Samuel and

Cissie here are paid on time. I mean, who are we to judge those who come here? We've all lived, haven't we?'

'Well, some of us.'

'Well, yes, perhaps not all of us.' Tabitha continued undeterred. 'They get a quart of good nutritious soup and half a pound of bread and butter. If Samuel remembers to boil the kettle there's sometimes a pint of coffee too. We experimented with stew after coming by a quantity of Australian beef, but it received mixed reviews – no reflection on Cissie's cooking,' Tabitha said, smiling at Samuel. 'You see, soup doesn't feel like charity but a square meal does, strange that, isn't it? We've a night school in the summer, a mothers' meeting and a sewing class, we're not just soup,' she said as if it were an advertising slogan or a line from a popular song. 'You'd be surprised by some of the desiderata here in darkest England.'

'And you come here every night?'

'Most nights, more often than not.'

'Since when?'

'Almost five years now. I came to donate some of Mama's clothes when we finally got round to clearing out her room. Feel I've rather taken it as far as I can, place runs smoothly without me. Come on, I'll introduce you to Cissie and the others.'

In the brightly lit kitchen a woman was cleaning mounds of potato peelings from a metal table, coils of mottled skin and stark white undersides. There was a circular pan rack from which hung jam pans and dented jugs. An old dresser pushed against the wall was stacked with soup dishes and tin plates.

'We've potato Monday and Tuesday, a broth on Wednesday. What is it tonight?'

'Carrot,' said one of the women.

'Carrot,' Tabitha repeated with a bright smile. 'We've ten minutes before we open, why don't we find ourselves a cup of something?'

'Rum?' asked Eloise.

'I was thinking tea.'

They sat on a wooden bench. A girl with a very red mouth, sore and wind-chapped, came to Tabitha's side and whispered something. 'Excuse me a moment,' Tabitha said, and made her way to the other side of the hall. Eloise surveyed the room; large and draughty, three long tables down the middle and behind them a serving hatch and kitchen, where women were busy preparing the soup. Samuel was carrying a metal pan and serving jug to the head of each table. A kerosene heater was struggling to warm the room.

'Some nonsense in the line, an argy-bargy. They get like that, sometimes, the ones who drink.'

Tabitha moved the cup around in her hands. She looked across to the children, who had been let in ahead of the queue, spooning soup from shallow tin plates.

'We take them to St Anne's-on-Sea once a year, the little ones, to camp, with one of the larger missions up the road – they look down their noses at us as we're non-evangelising.'

'You go with them?'

'Oh yes. The train journey alone is a great adventure for most. And they all come home half a stone heavier. I have this image of them racing up towards me on sand dunes, there must have been a hundred or more, all in their uniforms, cheering, slipping in the sand. Their small faces glowing red. In the evening we make cocoa, vats of the stuff, three bags of sugar in each, sing hymns at the campfire. You should visit St Anne's, they've the most wonderful Moorish pavilion and a ladies' orchestra who play twice daily.' Tabitha paused. 'Perhaps you would find it rather tame.'

A young girl came up and tugged Tabitha's shirtsleeve. Tabitha put her arm around her in a well-intentioned but slightly clumsy manner.

'I remember Mama making a donation to a lady from the Society for the Care of Friendless Girls,' said Eloise. 'I somehow got it into my head that the money would be used to purchase the friends for the girls, I wondered exactly how they went about it, if these friends were real girls who were paid for their services or if they were large dolls or mannequins donated as friends. I suppose we were friendless girls ourselves in a way.'

'Hardly. I think we had every advantage possible.'

*

New leaves, the colour of absinthe, cast a faint green light through the room. There was a rustle from the fire, which shifted and sank, then raindrops at the window blown from the branches outside. It had seemed an austere place in her father's time but was more chaotic now, piles of papers stamped Wright & Co.

'Yes, here it is,' Charles said from behind the desk. It had been taken down a week ago, a square of unfaded wallpaper behind him where it had hung. It showed a couple by a river, sunlight through trees, sections of red earth around the path. It had a sketch-like quality, but was full of soft, clear light and complex shadow.

'Oh yes, very pretty.' Eloise perched on the corner of the desk.

'Do you remember it used to be in the hallway?'

'Mind if I smoke, Charles?'

'The women were all smoking at Glazebrook's last weekend.'

She took a cigarette case from her pocket, tiny sapphires along the lid. She tilted it towards the light.

'Rather lovely, isn't it? Gift from Miss Montana. I had my heart set on something more discreet, but Bessie insisted. Bought it before we left for America.'

She drew a cigarette from behind the elastic.

'She's taking a party down to Cornwall next month.'

Eloise lit her cigarette and took the faintest of puffs.

'She has a notion true England is to the west. I told Tabitha she should join us.'

'Good luck,' Charles said, boyish for a moment. 'It's all we can do to have her come to Windermere. Her diary is fuller than many of my associates at Westminster.'

He sat down and lit a cigar with a series of clacks high in the back of his mouth.

'Committees, charitable bodies, the Mission, I may hope to stand for Parliament but your sister is making a play for sainthood.'

'From what Tabitha tells me you're a dead cert to be joining them – the parliamentarians not the heavenly host.'

Charles looked suddenly very serious as if her prediction might jinx the enterprise.

'Is that why you were down at Glazebrook's? He was something in the last government, wasn't he? What's his line on all this?'

She pointed to the newspaper on the desk. Framed by dense columns of text was an image of a man in a round hat with a waxed moustache and a long row of medals. He was holding a pistol and leaning on an exotic-looking sword.

'Balkan League squabbling. They've no stomach for war or any aptitude.'

'Really?'

'The Bulgarian tsar will emerge with a bloodied nose. Anyhow, none of this has any effect on the politics of Europe.'

He tapped ash onto the image, then pushed the newspaper into the waste-paper basket.

'By the way, when people ask, what exactly am I to say you are doing in Paris? I don't imagine you can still be studying, and you seem to withdraw fairly regularly from your account.'

'Charles, you know very well what I do.'

'I'm to say you are what, an … artist?'

'You are welcome to tell your associates I am the King of Siam for all I care.'

'No, I don't think I'll do that.'

Charles handed the painting to Eloise who squinted down at it, the cigarette pinched between her lips.

'Are you sure you want rid?' she said, blowing smoke towards the ceiling.

'I'm told it will fetch a decent price.'

'Mama was so fond of it.'

'It's to go, much to be cleared, now is the time.'

She watched the rain dripping from the branches outside; fat prisms catching the light, the greens of the new leaves.

'You know if you're in a predicament of some sort I'm sure Bessie could help.'

'I'm sorry?'

'Financially.'

Charles's face had suddenly fixed, the corners of his mouth turned down. He sat blinking as if attempting to flush something from his eyes.

'Eloise, I wish to be rid of a few old pictures. I was affording you the courtesy of viewing them before I did. You have never taken much interest in our businesses but I'd be very happy to talk you through a few aspects of their operation. We have three mills within ten miles of here, with highly specialised processes in each. We ship to Bombay and Shanghai. We have net capital expenditure … '

As Charles spoke, Eloise picked up a silver pencil from the desk and began cross-hatching on the back on an envelope. It formed an economical likeness of her brother. She shaded the dark knot of his necktie.

'Yes, Charles, you see, they are all simply words,' she said, putting the pencil down.

'What I'm saying is that should you need money – capital I believe you call it – then Bessie and her connections might be of use.'

'Have I not made myself clear?'

'Abundantly.'

She extinguished her cigarette, brushing it lightly against the ashtray.

'Rain's stopped. Think I'll take a turn around the garden.'

August

The window was covered by a wash of sandy grime. The sisters sat on opposite sides of the compartment, Eloise testing the seat's springs with her palms.

'I'm so glad you said yes, I know we'll have the most marvellous few days.'

Tabitha smiled, narrowing her eyes at the grain of condescension in her sister's tone.

'It's an awfully jolly crowd,' Eloise said, inspecting herself in a compact. She ran her tongue along her teeth then snapped it shut. 'There's Bessie, and Maud Watson, whose cousin married a Cunard, and a few others. Valentin will be there, of course,' she said with a counterfeit yawn, 'and a man called Fairclough Monthugh. Canadian.'

Tabitha continued reading as the train let out a whistle and the carriage shunted forward then stopped. Eloise saw the guard blow his own whistle then wave a flag as a man ran along the platform.

'He's an economist up at Oxford, a touch slow-living for the merry gang Bessie likes to surround herself with. I met him in Chicago where he came to dinner at the Palmer down on the lake. Monstrous iron-and-brick confection. Bessie adores it; silver dollars in the barbershop floor, giant lanterns by the Ladies' Entrance, you know the type.'

'I'm not sure I do,' said Tabitha, licking her fingertip and turning a page.

'He's not wealthy but I think he knows plenty of people who are – seems to represent their interests. What do you call that?'

Before Tabitha could reply the carriage gave a lurch forward and the people on the platform began to wave. Soon they were in open countryside, fields of rapeseed giving off a gluey-yellow shimmer.

'Did I tell you I had a note from Bessie when we arrived at the hotel last night?'

The hotel was a shabby affair a few hundred yards from Paddington Station. 'She said they are all excited to have us joining them. Mentioned you by name, said what a pleasure it would be to continue your acquaintanceship. Even sent her regards to our brother, which I thought gallant. Not one for grudges. Said she intended to send him something in recognition of his hospitality. Recognition – I thought that an interesting word.'

The lexical exactness had drawn Tabitha's attention. She looked up from her book.

'Yes, something of the battlefield about it, isn't there?'

'Distinguished service.'

'Valour in the face of the enemy.'

It was an hour before the sisters spoke again.

'What's that you're reading?'

'The story of one lady's life in Belarus and her subsequent journey to America.'

'I don't imagine she dined with the captain on her way over. Did I tell you Bessie threw a party one evening in her cabin? Had the quartermaster bring up a case of champagne. Word got round and before long there were two dozen of us crammed in there. A man was violently sick in her bathroom.'

Eloise rocked back in her seat, calculating something, hesitating, then looking directly at her sister.

'Would you like to hear a revolting story?' She folded one leg underneath herself and turned towards the window. Black trees flashed by, then a rolling set of open fields, a scarecrow, its stuffed head collapsed to one side.

'In Paris I knew of a man with a penis the size of a marrow.'

'Eloise!' Tabitha glanced to the closed compartment door, the corridor beyond.

'Well, I did,' Eloise said, relishing being so brazen.

Tabitha had broken into a blush down the side of her neck which Eloise took as signal to continue.

'He would take it out at parties and place it inside glassware. He told me that once a term the students at the Medical School would line up to see it under the guidance of a Dr Babinski.'

'Eloise, please,' said Tabitha, regaining a little of her composure.

'Colour of a jugged hare.'

Eloise took a small pocketknife and an apple and from her jacket, dissecting it into thin segments which she placed on a clean white handkerchief on the seat beside her.

'Have you ever seen one?' she asked as she ran her tongue along the blunt edge of the knife, eyes tightening at the tartness of the juice.

'A jugged hare? Yes, we had them for supper regularly in Windermere.'

'No, Tab.' Eloise paused, staring at her sister until her eyes met her own. 'A cock.'

Tabitha snapped her book shut and said, 'If you continue with this lewdness I will have to insist you move to another carriage.'

Eloise lifted the handkerchief with its sliced apple and offered it to Tabitha.

Outside a man was unsteadily making his way along the corridor.

'Now look, that gentleman is looking for an empty compartment,' said Tabitha, gesturing with a piece of apple. 'Should he prove unable to find one I suspect he'll join us. So no more talk of jugged hares or jugged anything for that matter. And tell me, Ellie, really, this costume of yours …'

'I'm not entirely sure what you mean.'

'The gentleman's jacket, the shoes.'

'Do you think it unladylike?'

'I simply wondered what it all meant.'

'I'm not really sure it means anything.'

Bessie was on the platform waiting for them. Eloise stood at the carriage window, leaning out as the train came to a halt. She waved at Bessie then turned back to Tabitha who stood with their suitcases.

'I hope she's brought refreshment.'

Bessie offered Eloise a hand down, then embraced her. She was wearing a smock fastened with a rustic leather belt and a set of jet beads, a scarf tied around her head like a Russian peasant. There were perspiration marks under her arms.

'Have you a porter?' Eloise asked.

'Bourgeois rot,' said Bessie. 'Fairclough was good enough to drive me down in the motor car I've somehow managed to acquire.'

Eloise glanced at Tabitha and grinned. She noticed Tabitha was carrying both their cases, unlinked Bessie and took her own case from her sister.

'Here, let me, fair's fair,' she said, relinking Bessie, leaving her sister to walk alone behind them.

Fairclough Monthugh stood leaning against the wheel arch of a light olive motor car. It looked very new and expensive. Before Bessie could introduce him to Tabitha, Eloise stepped forward and extended her hand,

'Hello, Fairclough.'

Fairclough folded his newspaper and wedged it under his arm. There were faint marks from the driving goggles around his eyes.

'Fairclough, this is Tabitha Wright,' Bessie said, gesturing to where she stood with the cases.

'My pleasure,' said Fairclough. He was a tall man with thinning sandy-coloured hair, a long nose with flared nostrils, the exposed septum glowing pink where the light hit it. He wore a pair of plus fours and a thick cotton shirt, sleeves rolled above the elbows. He had a slight tremor, Tabitha noticed, as he held out his hand.

'Quite the machine,' said Eloise, inspecting the wheels; pristine and glossily black.

'Engine blocks manufactured up in Newcastle, radiator in Wolverhampton. Remainder put together in a place you call God's Own Country. A dream to drive. Would you like to try?'

'Oh yes,' said Eloise who, before Fairclough could renege, had jumped into the driver's seat. Fairclough tossed her the goggles, removed a wicker basket from the boot, then secured their cases. He helped Bessie then Tabitha into the back, then passed the basket to Bessie.

'Crank her up,' said Eloise, fingers stiffening around the wheel.

'No need,' said Fairclough, climbing into the passenger seat. 'She's electric, switch is down there by your feet.'

'Oh my,' said Eloise, reaching for the switch, 'many a broken wrist averted.'

The engine fired up with a gurgling rattle followed by a pop from the back seat of the car. Fairclough let off the brake. Eloise glanced over her shoulder.

'None for you until we're home,' said Bessie as the motor car rattled over a steeply cobbled section of the road.

'Miss Wright?'

Before she could answer Bessie thrust a mug into her hand, splashing champagne onto her as she filled it. Eloise sounded the klaxon, causing a clergyman in a black hat and two boys pushing bicycles to scatter from the road.

After Eloise had navigated the cobbled lanes around the station, then the countryside between Halsetown and Zennor, by mutual agreement she brought the vehicle to a halt beside a field where women were harvesting strawberries, working along the sandy rows between low dense green bushes. Fairclough swigged the last of his champagne, then raced to the driver's side to take the wheel. Bessie noticed a sign for Rhubarb and insisted on being let out, telling them she would see them at the house.

'And who else do we have staying?' Eloise asked, glancing back to see Bessie, skirt hitched above her ankles, striding gamely across the field towards the farmhouse.

'Valentin, of course,' said Fairclough, hunched forward over the wheel.

'The Watsons?'

'No. Away. Europe.'

'And in their place?'

'Siddhartha Chatterjee and his wife Florence. Medical doctor. Forsaken the Hippocratic oath in favour of writing a novel.'

'What's he like?'

'Gives the impression of being terribly high-born. Bessie thinks his wife slightly, well, double-A S double-A C.'

'Double-A S double what?' asked Tabitha.

'Avoid at supper at all costs,' laughed Eloise.

'There's a couple from the Rhineland. Seem to spend most of their time swimming or in their room, get exceedingly drunk in the evenings, bicker terribly.'

'Oh dear.'

'Don't speak very much English — Bessie seems to communicate almost exclusively through mime.'

Eloise lit two cigarettes and passed one to Fairclough, who reached over without taking his eyes from the road.

'Who else?'

'The waifs,' he said, blowing smoke towards his window, 'between whom I find it almost impossible to distinguish. They're either sisters or lovers or runaways or some combination of the three. Bessie refuses to tell me anything about them.'

Fairclough glanced over his shoulder to Tabitha.

'Don't worry, Miss Wright, it's all much tamer than it sounds.'

'Any more?' asked Eloise.

'That's the lot. As far as I know. Oh, and Valentin is now a sculptor.'

As they turned down the lane towards the house they were met by high-sided hedgerows, a sense of the sea nearby, a subtle increase in the volume of light. Fairclough sounded the klaxon, sending dark birds scattering from the hedges. The party decanted themselves from the motor car, the metal engine parts condensing in pops and cracks.

'Oh yes, this is lovely.'

Eloise leaned against the bonnet, finishing her cigarette as Tabitha went through the lychgate and stood beside a wisteria with pendulous, pale violet stems. She cupped one and brought it close to her face.

'Poison,' Fairclough called out as he unloaded their cases.

Tabitha let go, looking embarrassed.

'Well, only mildly,' he said with a smile.

Fairclough led the sisters round to the back of the house where a semicircular lawn gave onto a steep sea cliff. There was a tall palm tree breaking into spiky heads, which had begun to brown and harden. Beyond the palm a precarious-looking set of steps, frayed rope for a handrail, led to the cove and the sea below, blue-green in the afternoon sun. In the distance there was a rocky island with a white lighthouse in need of repainting.

'Bessie has taken the place for three months,' said Fairclough, 'though from the way she talks about it, it's hard to tell if she thinks it quaint or faintly onerous.'

'How could such a place ever be onerous?' asked Tabitha.

'She claims the lighthouse keeps her awake at night.'

There was a croquet set abandoned mid-game, hoops bent back in the grass, bright balls clustered around the post. A man with cropped hair and a wiry chin beard, wearing a linen suit and a pair of hobnail boots, approached. He stopped to pick up a mallet.

'Mr Stock here is another of Miss Montana's protégés,' said Eloise.

Valentin Stock gave a shallow bow, turning the mallet upside down, using it to rest his weight on, suddenly dandyish.

'Mr Stock began life as a Futurist but is now an avowed Neoprimitive.'

'I'm not sure I know what either of those are,' said Tabitha, 'but it sounds a definite improvement.'

Valentin's pale eyes moved quickly over her.

'You are with us how long?' he asked in an accent Tabitha could not place. He began to pat his pockets, retrieving a crumbling, half-smoked cheroot.

'Five days,' said Tabitha.

He patted his pockets again, finding a box of matches. There was the sound of a vehicle coming to a halt outside. From where they stood they could see a lorry, dust settling around the wheel arches.

'My stone,' said Valentin.

*

Fairclough carried the stems of rhubarb into the house as Valentin spoke with the men from the quarry, gesturing with his mallet over to the stables. They set to work lowering the slabs of grey polyphant onto a barrow. When the driver approached Valentin with the invoice, he raised the mallet in the direction of Bessie.

Fairclough, back from depositing the rhubarb, said, 'Here, I'll take it.'

'Game old girl, ain't she?' said the driver, lifting his cap and running his sleeve along his brow. He had a chin of yellow-grey stubble, nose threaded with wide red veins.

'Flagged us down in the middle of the road. Gave me the fright of my life, one minute the lane was clear next she steps out from nowhere, waving her scarf. Good thing Clemo here spotted her. Can't say for certain I would have.'

'Good job indeed,' said Fairclough.

'There's three ton of stone on that thing,' said the driver, sensing he wasn't being taken entirely seriously, 'you know what the braking distance is for that, because she clearly don't?'

*

The wall's herringbone slates were dotted with sea pinks. Beside it there was a couple looking out towards the lighthouse, the woman pointing as the man shook his head.

'Mr Chatterjee, this is Miss Tabitha Wright and her sister Eloise, whom I have told you so much about.'

The sun obscuring his face. He hesitated before turning. He had very dark eyes and neat leonine features, a slight stoop, his black hair parted starkly and unpomaded. He was wearing a blue cotton suit, a pair of gold spectacles. He held a straw boater which seemed an encumbrance.

'Miss Wright, this is my wife Florence.'

'We were admiring the panorama,' Florence said. She wore a wide straw hat, under which one could just make out her face: its snub nose and small, slightly pinched mouth.

'Florence thought she saw a whale.'

'Darling, I'm certain I did.'

'Porpoise perhaps, whales I very much doubt,' Bessie said as if this were just the latest of many corrections she had been called on to make.

'Chatterjee is going to write the first great novel of our century.'

Chatterjee, abashed, looked down at his shoes.

'Oh do write me into it,' said Eloise, leaning to shake Florence Chatterjee's hand, then turning to curl a plume of smoke away from the party. 'But make me taller. A few inches. I should like to be as tall as Tabitha here.'

'Only in fiction,' said Tabitha at which the four women laughed and Chatterjee again glanced at his feet.

'He seems sweet,' said Eloise when eventually she caught up with Bessie.

'Sometimes,' said Bessie, 'he writes the most wonderfully caustic letters; serves them up *saignant* shading into *bleu*. None are spared. I'm thinking of sending him to Rome for a spell, escape that beastly wife of his.'

The sisters followed Bessie to a pair of deckchairs facing the lighthouse, damp outlines visible through the canvas. Bessie walked in front of the sunbathers.

'You've been swimming?' she said, miming a slightly frenetic crawl.

'Very much so,' said the man, realising there were others behind him and standing. Bessie signalled for Eloise and Tabitha to join her.

'Eloise and Tabitha Wright, Johannes and Eliana Althoff.'

Eliana stood now too; she was tall and athletically built. She wore a black mohair bathing suit, had strong pale thighs, and a sharp, sun-kissed face with thin lips. Beside her Johannes was more softly featured. The damp worsted of his bathing suit clung to his body. His bare legs were tanned and covered in coarse blond hair.

'Johannes is an aviator,' said Bessie, who mimed the uneven motion of an aeroplane.

'Die Fliegertruppen des deutschen Kaiserreiches,' said Johannes. He looked at Tabitha then let his gaze linger on Eloise, as if his lack of English made him somehow invisible.

'Claims he's the fastest man this side of Nova Scotia. First person to fly solo across the Carpathians — they're all clamouring to have him in one of their machines, isn't that right, Yoyo?'

It was unclear to the sisters how much of this he understood.

'Well, we shall leave you to your sun worship,' Bessie said, pointing at the sun for emphasis.

'An aviator? Really, Bessie, wherever did you find him?' said Eloise, linking her arm.

'The bar of the Carlton Hotel.' Bessie laughed. 'Old Mellon introduced us. I have to say they were slightly better value with a translator at hand. Chatterjee tells me that wife of his speaks a little German so she might be useful for something after all. Yoyo is a hoot. They're over for the Aerial Derby at Hendon, a hundred-mile circuit, Yoyo claims he can do it in an hour. Good luck I say.'

'Mr Monthugh mentioned there were two young ladies in the party?' said Tabitha.

'Ah yes, the waifs – you'll meet them later, no doubt.'

*

A steam-funnelled coal sloop was making its way westward across the bay. Tabitha's suitcase lay open on the luggage rack below the window.

'I thought there might be someone here to help us.'

'Help us do what?'

'Unpack. A lady's maid.'

'Bessie can't stand servants.'

'What do we know of Mr Stock?' said Tabitha, opening a drawer and unpacking from her suitcase.

'Bessie adores him, he can do no wrong in her eyes.'

'And in yours?'

Eloise shrugged.

'He speaks Italian, a little Russian, has an entire repertoire of Hungarian folk songs. I'm sure Bessie will have him serenade us after supper.'

'Where is he actually from?'

'That's just it,' said Eloise, taking a seat on the bed. 'No one knows. I heard a story he walked from Bucharest to Zurich as a boy. He lived in Vienna, then came to Paris where he was introduced to Bessie. He's been a fixture ever since. And he can't paint. Absolutely hopeless, hides his lack of technique behind increasingly opaque systems of belief. I think even Bessie has difficulty understanding some of them. Though she sticks by him. I'll be interested to see how his sculptures come out. Did you see he had claimed the stables?'

Tabitha had finished unpacking and now placed her case on the rack.

'You look tired,' Eloise said. 'I'll come and collect you before supper – Fairclough mentioned something about drinks on the lawn.'

*

The guests had congregated near the wall where a table was draped in a linen cloth; a dozen clean glasses arranged in a triangle. Siddhartha and his wife were talking to Johannes, Florence translating hesitantly. Fairclough greeted Eloise and Tabitha as they made their way across the lawn.

'Tell me, if I were to swim out from here where would I arrive?' asked Eloise.

'Kinsale,' said Tabitha, smiling at Fairclough.

'How disappointing. I see you've not dressed for dinner.'

'Took all my strength not to. Tomorrow we'll all be wearing gaberdines or sailcloth smocks or blouses with buttons like so many Pierrots, such is Bessie's wont.'

'At least you did the decent thing and put on fresh clothes.'

Eloise gestured to Valentin who had come from the stables unchanged since the arrival of men from the quarry, his boots covered in dust. He fished another part-smoked cheroot from his jacket.

'Well, here we are,' he said with a sigh, as if they were gathered to bury a shared acquaintance. 'No drink?' Fairclough shook his head. Valentin stepped up onto the wall and surveyed the waters of the teal-blue bay as Eloise greeted the Chatterjees and the Althoffs.

'Did you rest?' Fairclough asked Tabitha.

'Oh yes, thank you, rather too much, sound of the sea and all that, would have slept right through if Eloise hadn't woken me.'

Bessie came from the house carrying a bamboo-handled tray with a bottle of Italian vermouth, a bottle of Scotch, a jug of orange juice, and a large bowl of maraschino cherries. She was followed by a girl of sixteen or seventeen, whose hair looked as if it had been hacked away with something less precise than scissors. She was carrying a cork box of ice and wearing a sort of farmer's smock in indigo.

'Ah, smocks, Mr Monthugh,' Tabitha said, nodding at the girl. 'Perhaps you were right about tomorrow.'

Tabitha watched as the girl dropped the cork box on the table. At the door a second girl, dressed identically, with the same clumsily lopped hair, stood waiting. Bessie seemed not to mind the girl's departure.

'*Straub's*,' Bessie said, holding up a red leather book in one hand.

'Her new bible,' Eloise whispered to her sister, 'given to her by the wine steward at the Blackstone. We tried most of them on the boat over.' Eloise feigned nausea. 'Her favourite is the Jack Rose, named after some hoodlum she claims to have played cards with once.' The guests watched as Bessie poured generous measures of Scotch, vermouth then orange juice into the shaker. Eloise saw Fairclough whisper something to Tabitha who attempted to stifle a laugh.

*

In the dining room the ceiling was dissected by knotted beams; a warped lintel ran across the doorway and caused the taller members of the party, including Tabitha, to duck as they entered.

The table, which might have comfortably held six, was set for eleven. Bessie was laying out the last of the napkins, a green ginkgo leaf stitched on each. Johannes picked one up and fanned himself, grinning at Bessie as Siddhartha undid his collar and received a look of censure from Florence.

The temperature was raised by a candelabra burning with the long, liquid flames of cheap piano candles. There was another in the hearth, and another still at the window, where chintz curtains had been tied back to what, notionally at least, was a safe distance from the flames.

Tabitha was seated beside Fairclough, Eloise on the other side next to Valentin. The waifs were up near the head, by Bessie and Johannes; they seemed unbothered by the fact Johannes had turned his chair away from them to fully face Florence Chatterjee. Beyond the window, a faint trace of blue could be discerned in the rapidly blackening sky.

'I read polar explorers in peril have been known to eat their candles,' said Fairclough to Tabitha.

'I hope Miss Montana has something slightly more appealing on the menu.'

'Oh, I can assure you she has.'

'How can you be so certain?'

'When she wrote to invite me she insisted the condition of my coming was that I bring a cook. Thankfully we've a first-rate fellow at my college. We were at the harbour this morning buying crabs, but with Bessie, you never know, she may have dismissed the poor chap this afternoon.'

'Tell me, Mr Monthugh, what exactly is it you do at Oxford?'

'Well, this past year I've been seconded to the government – this business in the Black Country, have you been following it?'

'Vaguely.'

'It's an interesting story,' Fairclough said, pulling both his and Tabitha's napkin rings towards him. 'In May, the workers at a Patent Tube Works in a place called Wednesbury near the River Tame decided to cease work without notice. Quite the brouhaha. After negotiations with the Midland Employers' Federation, the union managed to secure a minimum twenty-three-shilling weekly wage.'

'And what was your role?'

'Well, I was called upon by the government to calculate what might happen if this were to repeat itself across the country. If every rubber works were to pay twenty-three shillings a week. It's remarkable, a fraction of a shilling, the difference it can make to all manner of things. Now I don't claim to be able to see the future, but I think I can get fairly close.'

'Is Mr Monthugh boring you, Tabitha?' Eloise called from the other side of the table. 'Is he telling you how he single-handedly averted the fall of the capitalist class?'

At Bessie's signal trays of dressed crab were brought out.

'Well, dig in,' said Bessie.

They had finished several more courses and good deal of wine when Bessie suddenly called out, 'Pig and Troughs.'

'Must we?' said Valentin, rolling his eyes.

'Past hour,' suggested Eloise.

'Chatterjee?' said Bessie.

Chatterjee removed his spectacles, wiped them on his napkin, then rubbed his eyes.

'Well, Pig, the crab, delicious. Trough, our aviator here being wooed by my wife.'

Johannes looked to Florence for a translation.

'I jest,' said Chatterjee. 'The only Trough is that it's perhaps a trifle warm in here.'

'Oh, an hour is far too dull,' said Bessie, after Eloise and Fairclough had both taken a turn.

'This past week,' said Bessie, seeking a broader frame of revelation.

'I think I can answer this,' said Tabitha, confident now she understood the rules. 'Waking from my rest earlier to the sound of the sea, absolute Pig.'

'Trough?' asked Fairclough.

Bessie gave a snuffling oink of encouragement.

'I don't feel I've really had the chance to talk to many of you properly.'

The party each took a turn. Florence Chatterjee was finishing describing her own Pigs and Troughs when Bessie cut across her and shouted, 'Whole entire life to date.'

'Oh no, Bessie, really,' said Eloise.

'This one generally ends in tears,' said Fairclough to Tabitha.

'And for God's sake keep them brief,' Bessie ordered. 'Valentin, you first.'

Valentin looked exceedingly put upon as if somehow demanded by the game.

'Peak,' he said and was met by a good-natured chorus of 'Pig!' 'Very well, Pig.' He thought for a moment. 'There is a bowl among the Moorish enamels at the Louvre, just beyond the staircase of the Assyrians.'

'Esoteric rot,' shouted Bessie. She hurled a bread roll across the table; it cannoned off Valentin's head and onto Florence's lap as she struggled to translate for Johannes.

'Chatterjee,' Bessie said, inclining her knife so it set a point of dazzling candlelight between his eyes.

'Swimming in the Hooghly with my grandfather.'

'Trough?'

'The day he retired from the High Court.'

'Eloise?'

'Far too many Pigs to mention.'

'Trough?'

'Cadaqués.'

Valentin affected then stifled a yawn.

'Careful, Valentin, I heard a rumour you're only here as Marsden Hartley is in Berlin,' said Eloise.

Valentin stabbed a finger into his wine then tasted it.

'And I have it on good authority that you and your sister are only here because a certain architect and his young painter friend couldn't be.'

'What are you talking about?'

'It's perfectly true, just ask Fairclough.'

Fairclough looked down at the table. Eloise stood, took her wine glass and hurled the contents at Valentin's face, soaking him and the whitewashed wall behind. He licked his lips thoughtfully, as if asked to identify the wine, pulling his damp goatee into a point. Johannes was laughing; even Siddhartha Chatterjee seemed amused.

Tabitha found her sister on the lawn. She sat on the grass beside her, shielding her from the house where the party continued undisturbed.

'Ellie, what is it? What's going on?'

Eloise dragged her sleeve across her face.

'He's a fucking swine, that's what's going on.'

She let out a deep sob. When she began to speak again it was in a very soft voice.

'Last summer we all travelled to a fishing village just over the Spanish border.'

Eloise glanced back to the dining room; someone was singing. 'We stayed at the home of an architect called

Borrell Cassals. There was a boy, Ramon, who would come to the house, a painter. We spent every day together. He took me walking in the cork trees at the Hermitage of Sant Sebastià. He showed me a set of frescoes he was being paid to restore. It was a source of such pride to him and his family. He seemed so pleased with his appointment, he was at pains to show me exactly how the work was progressing. He was committed, it was a calling.'

Eloise closed her eyes and turned her face up to the sky.

'You remember I'd planned to come home at the end of the summer?'

'I do,' said Tabitha. 'We were all so disappointed.'

'Well, this young man, Ramon, and I, we decided to go away. He wanted to show me the monastery at Sant Pere de Rodes. The house Bessie had taken had grown so raucous – you've seen how it gets. We took a train to Vilajuïga then a hired mule wagon to take us up to Alt Empordà. The journey was awful, bumping roads, pitiless sun.'

'Sounds like something out of Byron.'

'When we arrived at the village, the inn was shut but Ramon found us a house. There was a picture of St Ignatius above the bed. The bugs were horrendous, we would douse ourselves in powder every night. We stayed for two weeks. I remember it all so vividly; Ramon at the washstand or out on the balcony.'

Tabitha moved closer so their shoulders touched.

'He seemed so unaware of himself, of his beauty.'

'Ah, beauty,' said Tabitha. 'Dangerous.'

'Yes, well, it was actually. Terribly. We returned to Cadaqués, and I stayed on. That's when I knew. I could feel it.'

She placed her hand on her stomach.

'He refused point-blank to speak to me. I turned up at his house. In the end he sent his sister down. I lost my mind a little, I fear.'

'Why didn't you tell us? Why didn't you come home?'

'His sister tried to pay me to go away. Put a roll of banknotes in my hand. Told me I had no right stealing the boy's future. Told me he had been removed by the church from working on the frescoes.'

'Oh, Ellie.'

'Three weeks later in Paris, I was taken into the infirmary with pernicious anaemia.'

'Why didn't you say?'

'Bessie came with Valentin, and some girl from Guadeloupe who was modelling at the École. They were all still drunk, the whole thing was a joke to them. You see they don't care about anyone in the entire world.'

Eloise bit her bottom lip and suppressed a sob.

'Valentin became great friends with Ramon. Even had him come to Paris, paraded him around in a suit he had bought for him.'

'I say, you two, come back inside at once.'

Bessie came and stood looking down over the sisters, holding an empty wine bottle and a wooden spoon.

'If we all took offence at Valentin then we should never get through the day.'

Eloise got to her feet. It was as if she had completely forgotten the story she had just told Tabitha.

Bessie put her arm around Eloise's waist and said, 'Valentin is a very naughty boy and we shall make him pay, oh yes we shall.'

*

'Am I disturbing you?' Fairclough was wearing a pair of plus fours, argyle socks and a knitted pullover out of which his tie was poking. His hands were plunged into his trouser pockets. He looked very warm.

'Oh no, not at all,' said Tabitha, turning towards him. She was sitting under the palm by the wall, a fold-out picnic table draped in a paisley scarf. There were some books on the table and a sun-brittled copy of yesterday's *Times*. Florence had been reading with her until a few moments ago when she had gone inside to fetch a jug of water.

'I was actually looking for your sister.' Fairclough sat down in Florence's chair.

'I think she went crabbing with Bessie and some of the others.'

'Quite a bunch, aren't they?'

He took a pipe and a tobacco tin from his pocket.

'Bessie has a stout heart, if a rather short attention span. Her father was one of the founders of the Cincinnati Iron Company.'

'How did you come to know Miss Montana?'

'I met her at a supper seven, eight years ago. She was going about with a deerhound and two bull terriers at the time, wrote the next day to tell me how she appreciated my radical dryness of manner.'

Fairclough began thumbing a plug of moist shag into his pipe.

'You suspect there are better ends to which she might put that iron money.'

'I can't say I've given it a great deal of thought.'

'My theory is this.' Fairclough paused to light his pipe; it seemed to soothe his tremor. 'What happens here, in these, what shall we call them? Quasi-elevated places? Well, the spirit trickles out. I don't mean aviators or drunken sculptors, I mean, well, what do I mean? I suppose I mean the power of the artistic impulse to transform. I concede I am not on particularly firm ground.'

'I'm not sure what effect the goings-on here, pleasant as they may be, have on suffrage or the poor laws for that matter.'

There was a firmness to Tabitha's tone which did not seem to invite reply.

'It is rather opaque,' he said, taking the newspaper from the table. A bank of cloud moved across the bay, casting them in and out of shade. A gull, drifting down, landed with a jerk of its beak. It padded a few steps across the lawn, cawed, then broke into a lolloping run and took to the air.

'I hope my sister didn't embarrass herself last night.'

'Tame compared to some of the evenings I've witnessed. She's quite the talent.'

'We've always tried our best to support and understand her work.'

'You've a brother too, do you not?'

Fairclough took a handkerchief from his pocket. It was folded into a plump triangle; he rocked it against his brow which had begun to bead with sweat.

'That's correct.'

'Calicoes and whatnot, up north.'

He tracked the movement of the gull across the bay. It rose steadily then hung, body balanced between the black tips of its wings and the white triangle of its tail.

'That's him.'

'Well, I'm afraid that brother of yours may have some-what overextended himself.'

'I'm not sure I understand.'

'Loans,' said Fairclough, 'fairly sizeable ones. Your sister asked me to make some enquiries.'

'Enquiries?'

'I act as an adviser to the Institute of Bankers. William Deacon's, your brother's bank, is among their number.'

'Why are you telling me this, Mr Monthugh?'

She sounded girlish and hurt.

'I suppose I'm telling you because I can,' said Fairclough, inspecting the damp handkerchief then stuffing it back in the pocket of his plus fours. He stretched out his legs and crossed one wool-stockinged foot over the other. 'There's really no cause for concern. I should have made that clear.'

'So to be exact,' Tabitha said, trying to remain calm, 'my brother is in debt but his businesses are no way in danger?'

'Elegantly put.'

'How can this be?'

'Well, the bank will extend your brother's overdrafts in order to secure payments on the loans, I've no doubt about that. My grandmother in Manitoba had an English oak dresser my mother always coveted.'

Tabitha looked perplexed.

'Bear with me,' said Fairclough. 'When we came to move it in the days after my grandmother's passing – influenza, it was a bitter winter even by Manitoba standards – well, this dresser simply crumbled, just fell to pieces in our hands. What had seemed solid all those years was, at core, brittle as a wafer. It had been eaten clean through, you see, by powder-post beetles.'

'And?' asked Tabitha, sensing there was some connection to be made.

'Well, the banks as the debt holders keep the smaller specialist firms afloat, but this means the bigger operations are unable to secure the necessary efficiencies. Now the Lancashire Cotton Corporation may differ with me on this, but in my opinion the whole textile industry is bored through with unsound finance. Because of a freeze on wages, agreed by the cotton operatives, the industry appears in good health but just you remember that dresser back in Manitoba.'

'Are you suggesting my brother needs to do something?'

'If the Japanese make incursions into China and India, over time, it is reasonable to assume that the industry would require a wholesale restructuring, amalgamation of the smaller firms, such as your brother's, with larger outfits in the region. Though I doubt we'll see that happen.'

'What exactly is my brother to do?'

'Oh, nothing,' said Fairclough, 'continue as he is, the size of his firm means he is neither a drawer in the dresser nor a powder-post beetle.'

'What is he then?'

There was a crackle of nested tobacco, cawing from the gulls out over the bay.

'Perhaps he is an ornament on top of it, an *objet d'art.*'

'I am very confused, Mr Monthugh.'

'It's a confusing business. The dresser is rotten, of that there is no doubt, but so long as it stays where it is, and no one attempts to move it, all will be well.'

He uncrossed his feet, stood up, ran a hand through his thinning hair. His forehead had reddened in his time sitting beside Tabitha. He tapped out the scorched tobacco from his pipe onto the wall. Florence Chatterjee was coming back across the lawn, a jug of water in one hand. She raised it in greeting. Fairclough held his pipe up.

'I think I might walk down to the cove before lunch, see if I can't find those crabbers. Will you join me?'

*

After lunch, the waifs took over the picnic rug on the lawn, their long, angular bodies cast in full sun. One sat cross-legged, the other lay outstretched on her side. Their smocks stained white around their hems. They both looked very thin but something of the hardness in their faces disappeared close up.

As Tabitha approached them the girl who was lying on her side said, 'Oh, hello. I'm Inez and this is Carina.' She made a trailing gesture with the back of her hand towards her companion.

'How do you do, I'm Tabitha Wright. Are you twins?'

'Oh, she's not my sister,' said Carina, tearing up a clump of grass and throwing it ineffectually at Inez, who lightly brushed a few blades from her bare legs. Tabitha could see now, their hair and matching smocks aside, they looked quite unalike. Inez was darker, Carina broad-faced, Slavic-looking almost.

'You've been keeping to yourselves,' Tabitha remarked, taking a seat on the rug.

'We're being held against our will,' said Carina. She had a very husky voice, which made even speaking softly seem a great labour.

'We are practically prisoners, woeful, isn't it?' said Inez, sitting up, shielding her eyes, and taking a good look at Tabitha.

'I see,' said Tabitha. 'Have you been kidnapped?' She considered for a moment the possibility of Valentin arriving with them and some vague story about their origins.

'Oh no, we arrived of our own volition, more or less,' said Inez.

'And where is it you arrived from?'

'Why, St Petersburg,' said Inez as if it were the most obvious question in the world.

'That is a long way,' Tabitha said, unsure if she were being teased.

'We were at the Imperial Ballet School. Do you know it?' asked Carina.

'I don't think I do.'

'Ah,' said Inez at this.

'Inez here had a love affair with an Argentinian twice her age.'

'It was not a love affair, we exchanged three letters,' said Inez wearily.

'The fourth was intercepted by Madame Geltzer.'

'I see,' said Tabitha. 'And what led you to Cornwall?'

'We are here awaiting the arrival of her father,' said Carina.

'Apparently we couldn't be trusted in London,' added Inez with a hint of bitterness.

'And how did you become embroiled in all of this?' Tabitha asked Carina.

'I was acting as courier. I would collect the letters, you see, from the embassy where this fellow was an undersecretary.'

'Very junior,' Inez added for context.

'There was a physician on the next street I was seeing for my hip, well, for my buttocks, iliac crest and sacroiliac joint.'

'She was in as much trouble as I was.' Inez gave a soft laugh, rolled onto her back.

'I received a telegram from my father, telling me I wasn't to leave Inez's side.'

'I think they feared I was about to disappear. I'm not sure where, I have no money to speak of,' said Inez, herself now tearing up grass and throwing it up above her own face. She blew the fallen blades away then sat up.

'You don't happen to have a cigarette, do you?'

'I'm afraid I don't.'

'Liquor?' Carina asked hopefully, closing one eye. Tabitha shook her head. Both girls looked disheartened. Inez peeled off her socks; her feet were bruised, the toes rimmed with dry blood.

'And so how did you make your way here?'

'Oh, the train of course,' said Inez, whose interest in Tabitha had cooled.

'It was a hoot, well, to begin with,' said Carina.

'We travelled first class to Riga, told them we were countesses, but the money ran out at Vilnius; by Warsaw we were travelling third.'

'I'm surprised your father didn't send someone to escort you?'

'Well, I suppose he did.'

'Yes, a governess and then a private detective.'

'We tried to bribe her but she wouldn't accept it.'

'I offered her a very fetching brooch.'

'In the end we had to lock her in her hotel room.'

'The detective was trickier.'

'It would be untrue to say we evaded him fully.'

'Stern chap.'

'Played a great deal of solitaire.'

'Carried a blackjack, fearsome thing.'

'Rode with us from Łódź to Prague, which meant we ate at least.'

'We lost him in Prague then headed for Vienna.'

'I'm not sure if you girls are having me on.'

'It's all perfectly true,' said Carina.

'I suppose one of us shall have to write an account of it one day,' said Inez.

'And the detective?'

'Oh, he found us again in London, then he drove us all the way down here.'

'Trains are apparently too easy to evade him on,' said Carina.

'And where is this detective now?'

'He's staying at a boarding house in the village.'

'Calls in twice a day, to make sure we've not fled.'

'Oh, I'm finished with fleeing,' said Inez, lying on her back and bringing her bare feet stiffly together in the air.

'You're not here against your will too?' asked Carina.

'Oh no,' said Tabitha, 'not as far as I know.'

'Is that other lady your sister?'

'Yes, she is.'

'And what does she do?'

'She's a painter.'

'See,' said Carina.

'We thought as much.'

'And you?'

'I help to run a mission in Manchester.'

'Is that in London?' asked Carina.

Inez shook her head. 'Carina is an extremely graceful dancer, but she has nothing between her ears,' she said in apology, then added, 'That must be very rewarding.'

'I enjoy it.'

'Well, that's what matters, isn't it?' said Inez.

'And so how did you come to be in Miss Montana's care?'

'My father knows Miss Montana, the way one does,' said Inez.

'She's been much more pleasant than we expected,' said Carina brightly.

'I'm not sure why our fathers thought we would be better off here than in London, unless he hoped we'd drown ourselves.'

'And will you have to give up dancing?' asked Tabitha.

'Oh no,' said Inez.

'Inez intends to write to Fokine at the Ballets Russes, once all this has blown over.'

'Yes, dear Mikhail Mikhaylovich,' said Inez, 'he's been trying to get me out of my pointe shoes since I turned sixteen.' She tore a flap of dead skin from the ball of her heel, bit it between her eyeteeth, then tossed it onto the lawn. 'He prefers one to dance without, you see, he is exceedingly modern.'

'We saw his *Daphnis et Chloé* in Paris last summer with Papa,' said Carina proudly.

'Karsavina danced it like a pig in slippers,' Inez said. 'She may have made a good goatherd but never the shepherdess. One day dear Mikhail Mikhaylovich will realise this.'

'And when will your father be here?' asked Tabitha.

'Oh, any day now, I expect. He's sailing from New York.'

'Yes, and then –' Carina ostentatiously slit her throat with her index finger.

A biplane flew overhead across the bay. Johannes, who was drying off at the long wall, shielded his eyes with both hands and kicked Eliana's deckchair. Carina and Tabitha looked up. Inez seemed entirely unbothered by the appearance of the aircraft.

'Perhaps it's your Argie,' said Carina, throwing another handful of grass.

'Yes, how did your Argentinian friend take you having to leave?' asked Tabitha.

'He was going to teach you to tango, wasn't he?'said Carina.

'Alas, now I shall never know how.' She rolled over in a swoon, the pale underside of her forearm draped lightly across her brow.

'I have one more question if I may.'

'Go ahead,' said Carina like a bored duchess.

'Why is it you are dressed as you are? It's been a great subject of debate. Dr Chatterjee for example thought you were from the convalescent home in Truro and that your short hair perhaps signified a recent dose of measles.'

'Yuck,' said Inez while Carina inspected her arms as if mention of the illness might have given rise to an infection.

'Oh, we lost our luggage in Paris, a few days after giving that detective the slip.'

'Small price for an afternoon's freedom,' said Inez.

'We bought these in Pigalle.'

'Miss Montana offered to buy us new clothes.'

'Sweet of her, but we like these, don't we?' said Inez.

Carina nodded.

'And your hair?'

'We did that in Vienna. Inez thought we could sell it – at that point we were thinking of going on the lam, we weren't quite sure how one went about it, so we hacked it off with a knife there at the station and wandered into the old town.'

'What do you make of the troll?' Inez asked Tabitha.

'Chap with the goatee beard,' said Carina.

'Mr Stock.'

'Carina had a good look around his room.'

'Well, I was interested.'

'Tell Miss Wright what else you saw.'

'Oh,' said Carina, 'I saw the Indian chap making love to the Fräulein.'

'Dr Chatterjee?'

'That's the one.'

'We'd run out of tobacco, you see,' said Inez, 'so I sent Carina here on a little reconnoitre.'

'Trickier than you might imagine,' said Carina. 'Must have been midnight, perhaps a little after. First, I tried the troll.'

'Mr Stock,' said Inez.

'Over in the stables, had all these lamps hung around, offered me a glass of schnapps, didn't like the look of him, said no thank you very much, then I took a quick recce around the bedrooms, you were all still downstairs.'

'No luck,' said Inez.

'Then I remembered the Fräulein had been smoking before supper in the deckchairs.'

'So I sent her off to have a look.'

'He was reading to her, from a blue notebook.'

'Down towards the cove.'

'Saying something about how the words of his heart will be carried by the murmurings of a swan or perhaps it was the murmurings of a song.'

'He was clearly wooing her, you see,' said Inez as if this might be lost on Tabitha.

'Then he leaned in and kissed her on the throat,' said Carina.

'Very romantical,' said Inez.

'Thought it ill-mannered to linger.'

'Shame as the Fräulein had a whole box of Fanchez, which are absolutely first rate.'

'Are you quite sure it was Dr Chatterjee?'

'Oh yes, quite sure,' replied Carina.

'Keep it to yourself, I would,' said Inez, 'her chap seems a bit of a hothead, and it wouldn't do to cause a scene.'

*

That evening in the dining room Valentin and Johannes were playing a game which involved one of them slapping the back of the other's hands, as hard as they possibly could, until they missed and the privilege defaulted to the opponent.

Valentin's hands were webbed with fat bottle-green veins. Johannes's tapered with almond-shaped nails, cuticles oiled and pushed into supple crescents. As the guests arrived for supper the pair reluctantly desisted, the backs of both men's hands glowing a scalded red.

'Tabitha, you go there,' Bessie said, pointing to the head of the table. 'I didn't see you this afternoon?'

'Oh, no, I took a bicycle ride,' said Tabitha. 'Where are the girls?'

'Our waifs were collected earlier. I saw you talking with them. Do not believe a single word they tell you.'

'Well, the arguments are simple,' said Siddhartha Chatterjee. His teeth were stained with red wine. 'It is against God's will, it will destroy the home, and women cannot handle the responsibility because they lack any knowledge beyond the domestic sphere.'

'You can't possibly believe that,' said Tabitha.

'It's not a case of if I believe it or not, the silent majority need to be convinced.'

Siddhartha glanced at Bessie to ensure she was still enjoying seeing Tabitha provoked.

'Oh, enough talky-talky,' she said, snapping her hand like a long-billled bird. She looked over the candlelit scene, the empty wine bottles, the improvised ashtrays, the piles of fish bones. 'We need music.'

Fairclough was dancing with Tabitha, who moved rather stiffly. She had been pushed into his arms by Eloise who was dancing with Siddhartha Chatterjee, Florence with Johannes, while Eliana Althoff was waiting for Valentin to finish smoking a cheroot.

'You know, I thought you were very restrained back there,' Fairclough said, leaning towards Tabitha. 'History on your side and all that. Taxation without representation is, well, tyranny.'

Bessie changed the record, hurling the disc across the room.

'May I?' said Valentin, cutting in on Fairclough. The music started again. The smell of cognac was very strong on his breath. Tabitha had to turn her head away. Valentin pulled her towards him as she struggled to maintain distance between them. He had taken off his shoes and was dancing barefoot. She felt the weight of his head on her chest.

'Really, Mr Stock.'

Valentin looked up at her, his face was huge and far too close, and before she knew it he was attempting to kiss her. Tabitha gave him a hard shove below the shoulders with both hands. He staggered backwards, landing with a loud thump on the floor.

*

Tabitha woke with a headache and an extreme sensitivity to the light. It was pouring through the curtains at a quite unaccountable rate. She rolled onto her side and suddenly felt violently sick. She realised, with alarm, she was not wearing her nightdress. What was the last thing she could remember? There was a waltz she had reluctantly joined, Eloise as her partner. Bessie with a tennis umpire's megaphone, barking at the guests. A cocktail, streams of whisky, chartreuse, something bright blue, a colour which couldn't possibly occur in nature. Then toasts: Rabindranath Tagore, the Kaiser, Papposilenus; and when it had been Florence Chatterjee's turn to suggest someone she had hesitated and Bessie had called her a 'dumb bitch'. When Tabitha had attempted to leave, Eloise had grabbed her elbow, saying, 'Oh no you don't,' her mouth a slash of red. More dancing, the sofas pushed to the walls, a reel of some sort. She remembered Siddhartha Chatterjee crashing into a bookcase and Johannes grabbing Florence by the waist.

Tabitha heard breathing, a half-snore. It continued for a few seconds, the snuffle shortening until it stopped. She felt the blood draining from her face. A mosaic of memories began slowly to surface. There had been a game of sardines, started then abandoned, which was how they found themselves in his room ...

'Well, this is very.'

'Yes, well, very,' said Fairclough.

From downstairs there came an almighty clatter, breaking glass, and then the light metallic sound of a tray spinning to a stop on the stone floor. Out in the garden someone was shouting, 'Put that down at once.'

It was Bessie. Tabitha and Fairclough sat up, facing the window, the curtain pulsing softly. Before either could say another word, Eloise burst in. She seemed entirely unperturbed by the sight of her sister in bed with Fairclough. She ran towards the window then crouched, peeking out from behind the curtains. Wrapping herself in the bed sheet, Tabitha joined her. The pair looked down onto the garden.

Valentin was standing on the lawn. He was barefoot, shirtless. The wind had picked up, making a scratching sound as it passed through the desiccated branches of the palm.

'Put that down, you stupid ass,' Bessie said, fastening the belt on her dressing gown and striding towards him.

'Get back,' Valentin shouted, a heavy-looking pistol at his side.

When Bessie was about ten yards away, he raised the pistol and fired into the air, a dry crack, his arm recoiling awkwardly at the force.

'He's been up all night,' Eloise whispered.

Fairclough pulled on a pair of pyjama bottoms and came and joined them crouching at the window.

'Some girl has been blackmailing him. Threatening to tell his wife.'

'About the affair?' asked Fairclough.

'No, she claims she contracted the French gout.'

'French gout?' asked Tabitha.

'You know, the Great Pox.'

'I'm not sure I do.'

'For God's sake, Tabitha, syphilis.'

'He has a wife?'

'One would never guess from the way he carries on,' Eloise said.

Down on the lawn Bessie was moving slowly closer to Valentin.

'Now you listen to me, Valentin.' She was side-on to him, squinting. 'That thing is not to be played with. You put it down at once.'

Valentin shut his eyes and placed the pistol to his temple.

'Oh, you, stupid, stupid ass,' Bessie said, the last of her patience vanishing. She was only a few steps away. She turned full-on to him. Valentin's breath was shallow and fast, his body militarily straight. When Bessie was a step away, she dropped her shoulder and hurled herself at Valentin, sending him backwards with a jerk. There was a crack from the pistol as they fell to the grass. Eloise and Tabitha ducked below the window. There followed a long silence over which birdsong slowly asserted itself, the sound of the wind in the palm tree, the soft sounds from the sea beyond.

When they raised their heads above the window they saw Bessie and Valentin lying on their backs. Bessie let out a deep wheezing groan as if badly winded. She had one hand pressed against her ear. There was blood trickling down her wrist and into the sleeve of her dressing gown. She rolled awkwardly onto her side, dragged herself up on one knee, then stood, a finger hooped through the pistol's trigger guard.

Valentin lay perfectly still. It was only after a few moments of looking very hard that Eloise observed the faint rise and fall of his chest.

November

A slanted pillar of light fell through the hallway, dust motes, amber and ash-white, revolving in the beam. Charles stood before the mirror in his morning coat, framed by a pair of parlour palms. Beside him Claude was in church parade dress: dark blue forage cap, patrol jacket, trousers with their broad yellow stripe.

'At least an inch taller, I would say,' Claude said, laughing.

Charles tugged him down by the flap of his jacket.

'What are you, Papa, five foot three? Five foot four?'

He nudged his father and received a sharper push in return, which sent him stumbling away from the mirror. Charles's face remained dead straight despite Claude's laughter. The horseplay stopped as Hettie came downstairs. She stood between them, pinning a piece of heather to Claude's jacket.

'There's one there for you,' she said to Charles flatly. 'I'm sorry I can't be with you today.'

'It's fine, Mama, you should rest.'

Charles checked his pocket watch as the clock in the hallway released a brief flutter of chimes.

'Any sign of the others?'

'Upstairs,' said Hettie.

'What time are we to be there?'

'Eleven, I think,' said Claude.

'Then there's time for breakfast,' said Charles, who shouted up the stairs, 'For God's sake, do hurry along, Tabitha.'

*

Back at her desk, Hettie could hear voices in the hallway, then someone moving quickly on the floor above. She opened the edition of *Science and Health*. It was signed by Lady Victoria, whose own edition it had once been, and dedicated 'To Henrietta Wright, with love and in remembrance of all her healing work here in Manchester'. She had gone to the Bloodless Surgery after reading about it in the *Evening Chronicle*. Lady Victoria had been there, and her assistant, Miss Coutts-Fowlie, who had shown her into the reading room. The large, spare, rented space, none of the plush or gilt of the entrance hall, had just one table with a pair of chairs. Lady Victoria welcomed her like an old friend, taking her hand, inviting her to sit. Hettie had described her symptoms. The tiredness, the nausea, the pain in the legs and pelvis. Her loss of appetite. Lady Victoria had listened, hands spread on the table, head inclined as if she were absorbing Hettie's words into her very being. It could all be overcome, Lady Victoria assured her. She told her about her own healing, the righting of her spine and lungs, 'in India', she said, and then, 'Do you know India?'

Lady Victoria and Miss Coutts-Fowlie knew of Charles. They seemed determined to inform themselves of the entire city, as if the undertow of their healing work was a vast reconnaissance of what passed for society. Lady Victoria nodding attentively, Miss Coutts-Fowlie noting down a name or an address of what she called the 'sympathetic faithful', those who might contribute to the Bloodless Surgery or to the building of the Third Church planned in the south of the city. In the months that followed her first visit, Hettie had gone with them to the prayer meetings in Blackpool and Rochdale, to the lectures by Bicknell Young, the dapper former Mormon from Salt Lake City who had been miraculously healed in Chicago at the height of his career as a baritone and afterwards devoted his life to the Mother Church.

It was Bicknell Young who convinced Hettie she had it within her power to heal. 'The divine mind does not labour,' he said, adjusting his tie in the mirror, as they stood in his dressing room at the Albert Hall. He turned round to face her. 'It knows.' Lady Victoria and Miss Coutts-Fowlie, whose guest she had been, nodded in agreement. Then Lady Victoria said, 'We must give Mr Young some time to prepare. Thank you for receiving us so graciously.' He had given a low bow, then taken each of their hands in turn and kissed them. There were thousands packed into the audi-torium. People were being turned away outside. They had taken the train back to Manchester together that evening, Miss Coutts-Fowlie reading the passages of his lecture she had transcribed from their seats in the stalls close to the stage.

Hettie had begun her own healing with Esme. She had contracted polio at five. Her right leg was withered, she dragged it when she walked but took great pains to try and disguise it. There were other symptoms too, which had followed her out of girlhood. Esme would sit beside her on the bed, having been relieved of her duties for an hour each afternoon. They would close their eyes. Hettie saw bog cotton trembling in the breeze, a vast white wave spreading across the moor. After an hour of prayer, she would ask Esme about her symptoms.

'And your legs? What can you feel?'
'A tingling, here.'
Esme touched the top of her thigh.
'Stand for me.'

In August, when Eloise and Tabitha were away in Cornwall, Hettie had collapsed in the hall outside her bedroom. Dolly asked if she should call a doctor.

'I'll be fine in a moment. Please.'

She felt very weak as she looked down at her hands on the worn pink runner. She began to pray; Miss Baker Eddy, the bog cotton dotted across the moor moving in the breeze. Eventually she found the strength to crawl back to her bedroom. She spent the week there, insisting Charles did not call a doctor, sending her meals back to the kitchen, subsisting on prayer alone and little sips of water. In the morning Claude would come and refill the decanter.

'Please, Mama,' Claude said, 'you are not well, a doctor could —'

'Pray with me.'

'Mama, please.'

*

At breakfast, Charles held the newspaper out in front of him like a man playing an accordion. He was moving backwards from Monetary & Commercial. When he reached the front page he froze, his mouth a grim rictus, his lips very pale. Eloise reached and took the newspaper from him. The headline: MILITANTS CAUSE HAVOC. She began to read aloud from the article: 'The Cactus House at Alexandra Park containing a collection valued at over £50,000 was last night attacked ... Begbrook, a fine mansion near Bristol ... the pavilion of the Tennis Club at Catford ...'

'Is this the first you've heard of it, Papa?' Claude asked.

Charles thumped the breakfast table with the flat of his fist, then got up and left the room without answering.

'So much for those fabled powers of oratory,' said Eloise.

*

'Yes, well, ask him to call as soon as he can.' Charles hung the earpiece back on the brass hook.

'Any word?' said Claude. Charles shook his head.

'You cannot cycle to your own wedding, Tabitha, I forbid it.' Eloise was holding the train as Tabitha made her way downstairs.

'It was only a thought,' said Tabitha, her lower half now visible to Charles and Claude in the hallway.

'Damn silly one,' Charles called up, returning to the telephone.

'Your poor dress would be ruined,' said Eloise.

'I could change there, I'm sure.'

'No, it's all arranged, Benzie will drive us in,' said Charles.

Benzie had tied a white ribbon in a V on the bonnet of the waiting landaulet. Hettie hovered at the door, rubbing her shoulders against the chill. She waved stiffly as they pulled away.

They had been driving for only a few minutes when Charles said, 'Benzie, turn left down here.'

'Where are we going, Charles?' asked Eloise.

'Won't be long.'

'Oh, Charles, it's her wedding day.'

'Quick glance.'

'Charles, please.'

'Eloise, we've plenty of time.'

At the entrance a park-keeper and some children were standing by a man selling newspapers. Benzie turned in at the lodge and drove on past the propagating house and the bandstand, the black road sparkling from the recent rain.

'You know the way from here,' Charles said as they passed the sunken bowling green.

The glass was shattered in almost every window, leaving the painted wooden frame starkly exposed. Men were milling about in front, policemen and wardens in brown jackets, while others stood gazing up at the wreckage.

'Awful,' Benzie said.

Charles turned and looked at him as if an item of furniture had spoken. He glanced back at Tabitha, the train of her wedding dress carefully folded on the seat beside her. A policeman, clearly someone senior, approached the car. Charles lowered his window.

'Hello, Peacock.'

'Ah, Wright, hello.'

He was a tall man with a downturned mouth, a soft wattle of skin drooping over his collar.

'Residents in the houses over there were woken around four. A pipe we think packed with explosives, blew the railings clean off.'

Peacock gestured to a mangled twist of iron a few yards away. Men in cloth caps were pushing broken glass into piles with a shushing sound.

'Neighbours thought it had been snowing when they opened their curtains. Still awaiting a report on your cacti.'

'Anyone injured?'

'No word yet from Cobbald,' said Peacock, who then added gravely, 'We know he kept somewhat irregular hours.'

'If I can be of any assistance.'

'Good of you to look in,' Peacock said.

Charles nodded to Benzie who started the engine. As they began to pull away Peacock was approached by another officer who said something to him then pointed at the car. Peacock walked back towards them. He tapped on the passenger window.

'Miss Wright.'

Eloise felt Tabitha stiffen.

'May I offer you my congratulations?'

'Congratulations?'

Peacock looked at her for a long moment, then pointed at the train of her dress.

'He's a lucky chap.'

The rain had left dark marks along the ribbon on the bonnet. There was damp confetti in the gaps between the landaulet's seats.

'Do you think those people out there are thinking how on earth did that old girl manage to land herself such a handsome young lieutenant?'

'You're not that old, Aunt Eloise. Anyway –' Claude looked out of the window at the floating canopy of black umbrellas – 'you're not quite my type.' There was a brief silence then he said, 'It's very kind of you to see me off.'

'It's a pleasure – the chap they put me next to at lunch was awfully dull.'

She hesitated.

'You promise you'll take care of yourself, won't you?'

Claude laughed. 'It's a weekend camp at Caerwys, parading, marches, suppers with my brother officers. Very little can go wrong.'

In the stables at the barracks the geldings were restive, snorting and chomping in their stalls. There was wet straw spilled across the cobbles, a steaming pile of manure by the gate where Benzie had parked. A boy in a waistcoat walked past, a strong smell of beeswax and lanolin coming from the saddle he carried over one arm.

'I hope I'll see you before too long.'

'Come to Paris next year.'

'I should like that.'

'There are people there ... '

Claude seemed to colour slightly.

'I must go, Aunt Eloise.'

She squeezed his elbow. He snapped a brisk salute. A man wearing a combination of civilian and military dress, horse tack slung over his shoulder, smiled at Claude as he made his way into the barracks, mouthing something Eloise couldn't make out.

The landaulet moved along the wet streets. The tree trunks seemed much thicker than Eloise remembered, monstrous almost, rupturing the pavements, their foliage dense even now in early winter, as if the villas of her girlhood and their overgrown gardens were in the process of being reclaimed. Lichens dappled the coping stones, mosses flourished where the house names had been cut into their posts.

'She wants the place back, doesn't she?'

'Who's that, miss?'

'Nature, all these mansions, with their pretty gables and painted gates.'

Benzie nodded.

'I wonder if it'll all be forest again one day or a swamp.'

'Oh, I should think so, miss,' said Benzie, 'one day.'

It was very quiet back at the house. In the drawing room Hettie was sitting under blankets in a chair by the fire, like an animal in the early stages of hibernation.

'Did Claude get away safely?'

'Oh yes, all fine.'

'Did he look very dashing?'

'Very,' said Eloise.

'How was the service?'

'Mercifully short. Fairclough wore a black frock coat with a white boutonnière.'

'Did they give you anything to eat?'

'There was a lunch, duck. Tabitha sent the leftovers and most of the wedding cake in a motor taxi to the Mission.'

'Where are the others?'

'They decided to take a turn around the botanical gardens.'

'I've something for you.'

Hettie rose from her chair and made her way to the back of the room. She returned with a cardboard tube. Inside was a copy of the *Christian Science Sentinel*, on the cover two women set against Greek columns, beneath them an address in Boston to which all correspondence should be directed.

'Really, I mustn't deprive you.'

'I ordered two. Should you enjoy it, you'll be able to pick a copy up in the United States. I hope you will.'

'Yes, well, thank you,' Eloise said, taking the magazine. She pictured Bessie tossing it from the window of a moving motor taxi.

'The house will be a good deal quieter without you and your sister. I didn't imagine I would outlast you both, but there you go.'

She gave a faint smile which seemed to take a great deal of energy and concentration and which left her looking depleted.

'Do look at it closely,' she said. 'All manner of marvellous things in there. Yesterday I read of a man who was suffering from oesophageal cancer. Do you know why?'

Eloise shook her head.

'Because he believed in the material world. It's an illusion, you see. All of it. Do you understand?'

Eloise nodded. It seemed to please Hettie.

'I knew you would.'

Hettie made her way into the hall then up the stairs, pausing for breath.

'You leave tomorrow?' she said over her shoulder.

'Yes, for –'

But before she could finish, Hettie had turned her back.

'Arizona,' Eloise said.

It presented itself in her mind as blocks of colour and unadulterated light. She looked around the room and tried to fix it as it was, the clocks, the piano, the ammonites on the mantelpiece. It had begun to rain, lightly, at the window, on the rose stems trained beside the glass.

*A*t 19.00 C Squadron attached to the III Corps left its reserve billets at Lamotte-Warfusée on the Amiens–St Quentin road heading for the front at Estrées. At 23.55 Lt Wright led a patrol to the south of Tincourt Wood. Lt Wright was accompanied by two men, Sgt Maguire and Pte Reynolds. As far as can be ascertained, the patrol lost their way and encountered a German picket where they came under sustained fire. Lt Wright received wounds to the abdomen and shoulder. Sgt Maguire remained with him until dawn when he was ordered to return to lines and fetch help. A search party was sent out but regrettably no trace of Lt Wright or Pte Reynolds was found.

War Diaries, Duke of Lancaster's Own Yeomanry

ACKNOWLEDGEMENTS

I am indebted to Sarah Chalfant and Alba Ziegler-Bailey at the Wiley Agency, Alexandra Pringle, Allegra Le Fanu, Sara Helen Binney and Ros Ellis at Bloomsbury. To friends and first readers Will Goodlad, Edmund Gordon and Joe Stretch. To Karen Kennedy, Gwyneth Stringer, Sos Eltis and Keely Fisher, and to Andrew Motion, Robert Hampson, Jerome de Groot and Kate Williams who all, in their own way, helped shape this book. To Katherine Fry and her fine-toothed comb. To the Manchester Writing School and MMU, in particular Carol Ann Duffy, James Draper, Jess Edwards, Berthold Schoene, Sharon Handley and Malcolm Press. To Oli Wilson for finding a path across the moors, and to Christine and Martin Love, for the loan of their house with its view of the mountains. Finally, most of all, to Hannah, Gabriel and Felix for making life as rich as any fiction.

A NOTE ON THE TYPE

The text of this book is set in Fournier. Fournier is derived from the *romain du roi*, which was created towards the end of the seventeenth century from designs made by a committee of the Académie of Sciences for the exclusive use of the Imprimerie Royale. The original Fournier types were cut by the famous Paris founder Pierre Simon Fournier in about 1742. These types were some of the most influential designs of the eight and are counted among the earliest examples of the 'transitional' style of typeface. This Monotype version dates from 1924. Fournier is a light, clear face whose distinctive features are capital letters that are quite tall and bold in relation to the lower-case letters, and *decorative italics, which show the influence of the calligraphy of Fournier's time.*